AGE OF END:
THE RAT COLLECTOR

AGE OF END: THE RAT COLLECTOR
by Chris Yee

ISBN 978-0-9973536-1-7

Cover designed by Rebecca Frank
http://RebeccaFrank.design

Published by To The Moon Publishing
www.tothemoonpublish.com

ONE

VINCE WAITED AS the sharp cold of ice stabbed at the bare flesh of his feet. He stood atop an icy cliff, toes curled over the edge. His eyes scanned the horizon, waiting for Saul. Below him, a far drop to certain death.

He rocked from side to side, his arms twisting tightly across his chest. A snowflake gently landed on his nose and quickly melted. He looked up. Dark clouds. More snow was on its way. He grabbed his hood and draped it over his head. His eyes carefully panned across the lifeless snow covered plains, looking for movement. There was nothing.

His knees trembled, not from the cold, but from the anticipation. He knew Saul would arrive from the west, he just did not know when. His legs ached, and his body was tired, but he remained patient. This was too important to get overzealous. Lives depended on him.

The stinging pain residing in his feet had transformed into complete numbness. He tried to wiggle his toes. Wiggle. Move. Do anything. But it was pointless. He could see his own feet pressed against the ground, but it felt like they didn't exist at all. Like he was hovering over the frigid ice. His feet had once endured the fiery sands of deserts and traversed the jagged trails of mountains. Over the centuries they had grown resilient to many things, but the cold was new. It was far worse than he expected.

The sun, still blurred behind a sheet of clouds, lowered. Vince watched the dimly lit orb approach the flat ground. The sunset was comforting, perhaps too comforting. Nightfall would only bring colder winds. His pupils shrunk and his brows lowered as he mindlessly gazed at the ball of light. There was something soothing about the slow movement of the sun at the end of a long day. Something calming. Therapeutic. Hypnotic. With a cold breeze slapping his face, he snapped out of his daze and returned his attention to the snowy field below.

The spot Vince chose was not ideal, but it would serve his purpose well enough. He hoped for a place with more cover, more places to hide, but the area was void of any trees or vegetation, and the snow plains were extremely flat. Given the circumstances, the mountains were his best option. He settled at the edge of a cliff, a good distance from the main trail. The ice he stood on felt thin, but it held his weight, for now.

He glanced back at the fire he built. It had burnt out hours before. Time had passed quickly. Saul should have arrived by now. He considered building a new fire but decided it was more important to stay put. Focus his attention on the horizon. Come nightfall, a fire would only ruin his night vision, and worse, reveal his position. As tempting as a warm, freshly crafted fire was, it was a bad idea. He closed his eyes and imagined the warmth that radiated against his back when the fire was once fresh, but it only made him colder.

The thought of confronting Saul worried him. Too much time had passed since they last spoke. That terrible day from his childhood, still crystal clear in his mind. He was not quite sure what to expect from Saul now, but he was prepared for the worst. Saul was once a good friend, but he would not hesitate to kill him, if necessary.

The last rays of light stretched across the vast plains before disappearing beyond the horizon. The sun's afterglow remained for a short moment, and then slowly died away. The night was dark, but his eyes adjusted quickly. The cold grew colder. Flaky cracks spread across his lips. His nose was stuffed with mucus. Thick puffy clouds left his mouth with each breath. His dry throat scratched like cold sand. He reached for his canteen, but then remembered it was empty.

He bent over and formed a small pile of snow with his hand. He cupped the pile and packed it into a loose ball. It would make him colder, but his canteen had run empty days ago. He needed water. He stuck some snow on his tongue and pushed it against the roof of his mouth. The snow melted almost instantly. He let it settle in his mouth, on his tongue, against his cheeks, and then finally swallowed. He took the remaining snow, which had already melted, and rubbed his lips. He was still thirsty, but it would do for now. Consuming more snow would drop his temperature too much. He needed to stay warm. The cold night had just begun.

On him, he had a small bag of dried meat. His stomach growled, begging to be fed, but he was saving what little food he had for a later time. He would need the boost in energy when Saul arrived.

The rest of the night was uneventful. It snowed. Vince waited. Hours felt like days in what was perhaps the longest night of his life. *He will come*, Vince repeated to himself. *Saul will come*.

*****

Hope returned when Vince saw the blue morning sky. The harsh night was through. The dark clouds had cleared overnight, ending the heavy snowfall. The sun shined upon his skin. It was refreshing after a night of frigid air. Light stretched across the landscape, unveiling a beauty that was once hidden with clouds. There was still no movement in the fields below. Vince began to doubt if Saul would come at all. Was he wrong? Had Saul taken a different route?

A flock of birds flew towards him in the distance. The first sign of movement. His eyes followed them as they approached. When they finally passed over his head, his eyes darted back to the horizon, fully alert. The white field remained clear and uneventful. Still he watched. But there was nothing. His anticipation began to fade. Maybe Saul was not coming after all…

Something emerged in the distance. Vince strained his vision. He could see the top of a wool hat, bobbing up and down as the man wearing it walked towards him. A face slowly revealed itself. White, bushy eyebrows. Wrinkled cheeks. Long, crooked nose. Vince hadn't seen Saul in a long time, but he immediately recognized him. He looked weak. Old and fragile. Not at all what he expected, but it was most definitely him.

His heart rose to a pounding thump. No more waiting. He needed to get ready. From his bag, he removed the dried meat and stuffed it in his mouth. He ran over to the remains of the campfire and scattered the coals, covering them with snow. As he trotted back, the ice shifted. He stopped. Very carefully, he shifted his weight back and forth. It seemed stable enough. He tiptoed back to peer off the ledge. Saul was already at the base of the mountain, making his way up the trail. Vince pulled a large white sheet from his bag and spread it out on the ground. He dropped to his stomach, facing the trail, and folded half the sheet over himself. He peeked his eye out of a small hole, to keep sight of the trail.

Every muscle was tense, but he remained calm and still. He was a good distance from the trail, and he was well concealed. The overnight snowfall had covered his footprints. He was completely hidden to anyone passing by.

As he waited, he fought the urge to sleep; something far more challenging now that he was lying on the ground. His eyelids drooped, bounced up, then drooped again. He shook his head and focused. These next few moments were too important to sleep through. If Saul slipped by, people would die. It was as simple as that. But his body fought against him. After several days of no sleep, he finally gave in…

…He flinched awake. How much time had passed? It could have been hours, or seconds, or anywhere in between. Did he miss Saul? There were no footprints on the trail. A hopeful sign. He would wait a bit longer, now rested and alert.

After a short minute, footsteps grew from soft muffles to loud crunches. Adrenaline shot through his veins. He saw no one on the trail, but he could hear Saul approaching. He waited…eagerly.

Saul entered his sights. His body was frail as he struggled up the path. Vince was struck with awe. There he was. His old childhood friend. Seeing him up close was overwhelming. Yet, it was also underwhelming. Vince expected a towering menace. Someone who lived up to the terrifying stories. He expected a beast, but what he saw was a bug.

Saul stopped, taking a moment to rest. Vince only stared, not moving a single muscle. Saul started walking again, and he realized he was about to miss his opportunity. He sprung up from the ground, throwing the white sheet in a wild flutter. His feet thumped against the snow as he sprinted towards Saul, full speed.

TWO

S AUL WANDERED THE endless fields of snow. There was no life. No animals. No trees. Nothing but flat plains. The bland sameness of everything made it difficult to keep his bearings. Only the sun guided him, and today it chose to hide behind thick clouds. The cold was worse than he had expected, but it was tolerable. The delicate touch of a snowflake tickled his balding head. He searched through his bag and found a wool hat, wrapping it snugly around his head.

He had journeyed through snow for several days now, knowing that Vince followed closely behind. Vince's efforts to stay hidden were impressive but unsuccessful. Yet just a few days prior, he seemed to have vanished completely. It was strange. Vince was persistent. His sudden disappearance was alarming.

The cold was bearable, but not at all pleasant. He was glad he brought a pair of boots. He wondered if Vince had done the same. Walking barefoot in the snow for several days could cause serious damage to the feet.

It was a long eight days in the snow, but he was not fatigued. His muscles, while slender, were durable. His mind even more so. He had the energy to walk eight more days if necessary. He kept a steady pace, watching each step crunch in the ankle-high snow. His shadow stretched out front and faded into the oncoming darkness as the sun lowered over his shoulder.

Time was forever morphing. Some days passed in a blink, and others dragged for ages. Fortunately, today was the former. The day went by so fast he almost forgot to eat. He retrieved a bag of dried meat and stuffed a handful down his throat. He had plenty of food and water; enough to last another week. After gulping a generous portion of water, he grabbed another handful and devoured it.

The night was uneventful. It snowed. Saul walked.

*****

Dawn approached, and Saul's pace remained steady. The snow stopped overnight, and the sun was now peeking up from the horizon. Piercing rays of light shot off the snow and into Saul's eyes. It was far too bright. He lowered his head and watched his feet as he walked.

With his head down, he found himself surrounded by large birds. There was a full flock gathered in a small circle around him. He stopped just short of crushing a bird's head under his colossal boot. The feathered critter pecked and pulled at the tough leather. Saul smiled at the harmless creature. He stepped back, placed his thumb and index between his lips, and blew. The whistle sent the birds fluttering.

He watched them fly away and then carried on. The sun was still unbearably bright, but it faded quickly. He raised his head to see the large mountain range up ahead, rising up to block the sun as he walked forward. The sight was both aggravating and refreshing. Scaling the mountain would be tiring, but it was nice to see something new. Something other than flat fields of snow.

A trail sat at the base of the mountain, directly in front of him, snaking up and over the peak. It was his only way through. He increased his pace with unexpected enthusiasm. When he reached the mouth of the trail, he gazed up at the long path ahead. He took a deep breath, sipped some water, and stepped onto the trail, walking at a deliberate, steady pace.

After two hours, he was still at it. The incline was challenging, but he was managing well. He stopped for a short rest and glanced back to admire his progress. He was a good way up and was nearing the peak. Stepping forward continue his climb, there was the sudden fluttering sound, followed by rapid thumping. He turned, and froze, staring into the face of the man vaulting towards him. It was Vince.

THREE

VINCE SPRUNG UP from the ground, throwing the white sheet in a wild flutter. His feet thumped against the snow as he sprinted towards Saul, full speed. He saw shock in Saul's face. Saul turned and watched as Vince approached in a blaze of fury.

The breeze built to a strong gust. Vince pumped his legs faster and faster. His pounding heart matched the thump of his feet on the snow-covered ice. Thump. Thump. His eyes locked on Saul. Thump. Thump. Thump. Saul stood, unable to move. Thump. Thump. Thump. Thump…

A loud crack echoed through the air as the ice supporting him shifted again. He leaped forward as the ice snapped off. He soared through the air, arms extended, fingers stretched. He could almost touch Saul, but not quite.

He plummeted past his friend and slammed into the side of the cliff, bouncing off the ice and back into free fall. His body spun violently. The deafening wind slapped across his face. He adjusted his arms to stop the spinning. Below him, the platform of ice had shattered into small shards and was falling in pieces. In front of him, the rough cliff face whizzed past his head as he hurtled down towards the ground. He reached his hand out, touching the jagged ice with his finger. A vicious pain shot up his arm.

He drew a knife from his bag, gripped it tightly with both hands, and raised it up over his head. When he thrust the blade into the ice, it cut through with ease. The upward pull swung his body around and slammed his torso into the hard surface. His arms pulled up as he held his grip, but his momentum pulled down. His shoulders felt like they would rip out of their sockets. His body stretched out with excruciating pain. It was a pain he could endure. He just prayed the knife would as well.

As he dragged down the side of the cliff, he pressed his feet against the wall to alleviate the stress on his shoulders. The skin on his soles tore off in chunks as they scraped against the uneven ice. Blood streaks smeared along the wall as he slid down. His feet were numb, so he felt no pain, but he cringed at the sound of his own tearing flesh. His descent slowed, and the stress on his shoulders lessened, until finally, he came to a stop.

He sighed with relief and let his feet dangle over the vast nothingness below. Thick blood oozed from his toes. Still gripping his knife with one hand, he reached for his bag and pulled out a second one. It was his father's. Old and beat up, but still durable. He struck the ice with the dull blade, but only partly broke the surface. With a few more strikes the knife was firmly planted.

He pulled himself up and rested on the stump of the handle, leaning against the other for balance. There were two options. Climb back up to the spot where he fell, or climb down to the base and walk up the trail again. Going up would be far less trouble.

Slowly and carefully, he folded his leg over to look at the damage. His soles were completely shredded. Blood gushed from large chunks that were torn off. An intense dizziness washed over him, and he leaned against the knife so as not to fall. He was losing too much blood. He ripped off strips of his coat, forming long rags, and wrapped them tightly around his feet. The light brown cloth quickly darkened to a deep crimson.

He carefully lowered his body back to a hanging position. Using both knives, he climbed his way up, stabbing the ice hand over hand. When he needed to, he took a short break. The hollow winds chilled the air and dried the sweat from his brow.

Nearing the top, he took one last moment to rest. The bandages on his feet were now sodden with blood. Thick fluid dripped from the saturated cloths. A strong headache crept up and progressively worsened. He panted heavily, grasping for whatever oxygen was left in the thin mountain air.

When he reached the top, he slammed both blades into the ground and used his last bits of energy to pull himself over the edge. He laid on his back, looking up at the sky. His arms splayed across the snow, and his chest vigorously pumped up and down. He lifted his head to look around. As expected, Saul was gone.

He sat up, grabbed both knives, and placed them back in his bag. Attempting to stand up, he stumbled and fell to the ground. He tried again, but his mind was overwhelmed with dizziness. He fell again, this time slamming his cheek against the ice. The last of his energy seeped through his skin and his body went limp. The white snow turned to black as his eyes rolled back in their sockets.

FOUR

L ET'S STOP HERE for a moment," Rupert said. Fred gave him a puzzled look, "I want to stretch my legs."

He dismounted his horse, gently digging his boots into the heavy snow. Fred watched in silence as Rupert stretched. She was perched atop a thick pad on Rupert's right shoulder. She was a falcon and an excellent hunting bird.

At a young age, Fred was separated from her mother and came dangerously close to death. Luckily, Rupert spotted the helpless young bird and nursed her back to health. Of course, her name was not initially Fred. Rupert had no name for her. He was awful with names. He brought her back to Snow Peak, where the children were ecstatic about their new pet. They threw names back and forth, and eventually landed on Fred. They later discovered that Fred was a female falcon, but the children insisted that she had the face of a Fred, so the name stuck.

Over the next five years, Fred became close with Snow Peak and its dwellers. They loved her, and she loved them. She was especially fond of Rupert. He decided to train her in the ways of hunting. He noticed her strong hunting instincts early on. She had keen eyes and sharp talons, perfect for tracking and killing prey. She learned quickly, showing off her impressive skills after only a few days, and she very much enjoyed it. Maybe it was animal instinct, or perhaps she just liked showing off. Fred was a pompous, arrogant bird, after all, ...in the best possible way.

So as Rupert dismounted his horse and dug his boots into the snow, Fred displayed a burning confidence. Today was the season's first hunt day. They usually went to the woods to hunt, but this time, they tried the snow plains. He looked around and observed his surroundings. To his right, the endless snow-covered plains. To his left, the large mountain range. He had never crossed over to this side of the mountains before. The hunting trip was a good excuse to explore these new grounds.

"Okay," he said, as he mounted his horse. "I'm all stretched out. Let's go." They galloped along until the mountains were out of sight. Now there was only flat snow all around. He pulled on the reins and dismounted again. "This looks like a good place to set up camp." He reached for his bag and began to unpack.

As he worked on the camp, Fred watched from a lonely tree stump nearby. Rupert pitched the tent and built a fire using logs they had brought. The cold would worsen come nightfall, and snow was on its way. If they wanted to get through the night, fire and shelter were necessary. Anything else was a luxury. When the modest camp was complete, Rupert took Fred's spot on the stump, and Fred returned to his shoulder. It was time to hunt. They both peered off into the horizon, waiting for movement. Fred was ready to pounce.

Before sundown, Fred had gathered twenty kills. Satisfied with her performance, Rupert called it a day. They huddled in their small tent as the sun lowered, and the wind and snow picked up.

"You did well today, girl." The wind howled outside as Rupert spoke. "We'll hunt a little in the morning and head back by noon. We should be back to Snow Peak by sundown." Fred responded with a blank stare. "You know, you're good company, but sometimes I wonder if you understand a single word coming out of my mouth."

They slept undisturbed, Rupert on the ground, Fred perched in the corner. Their tent blocked the harsh weather outside.

*****

By morning, the snow stopped, and the wind lessened. The sky was clear and blue. Rupert and Fred awoke at sunrise, spending the entire morning hunting. Satisfied again with Fred's performance, he decided to call it a day. He marched back to the tent, as Fred relaxed on his shoulder, admiring the scenery. In the distance, she saw a small cluster of birds. She sprung from Rupert's shoulder towards the flock to investigate. And maybe to kill.

"Fred!" Rupert yelled, "What are you doing? Come back here!"

She ignored him. Her wings spread out wide as she glided with confidence. Her eyes locked onto a single bird. The wind roared past her head as she gained speed. Her talons opened, ready to snatch her prey, when suddenly, a mysterious figure emerged from the horizon. A man.

Her wings went stiff. Her heart raced as she stared at the approaching man. Something about him struck fear into her very soul. Her head spun in circles as she tumbled into the snow.

She quickly recovered and jumped back into flight, headed in the opposite direction. She fled towards the protective hands of Rupert. Rupert caught her and immediately knew something was wrong.

"What is it, girl? What did you see?"

He looked up and caught sight of a man wearing a black coat and wool hat, marching through the snow. He dashed back to camp, collapsed the tent, placed Fred on the ground, and laid on his stomach beside her. He stayed low and watched the man, who was now standing among a flock of birds. A loud whistle cut through the silence, and the birds fluttered away.

The man continued walking in the direction of Snow Peak. Rupert hopped to his feet and packed the rest of their luggage, making sure to stay low. When he finished, he glanced back. The man was gone. There were fresh footprints leading towards the mountain range. Rupert mounted his horse, and Fred returned to his shoulder.

They galloped along until the mountains were in sight. Rupert could see the mysterious man at the base of the trail. Rupert approached the mountain, moving slowly to keep his distance. As he got closer, a hollow crack echoed from above. His eyes darted up. A large section of ice tumbled off the mountainside and crashed to the ground.

They rode up the path, both curious and cautious of what happened. Who was this man and why was he here? When they reached the top, they did not find the man they expected. Instead, they found someone else, lying helplessly in the snow. Red footprints climbed up and over the edge of the cliff, leading straight to his bloodied feet. His eyes, wide open, were rolled back in their sockets.

Rupert dismounted and approached the body with caution. Fred flew over and landed on the side of the stranger's head, looking down at his face. She twisted her neck and curiously pecked his cheek, breaking the skin. A thick drop of blood trickled from the small cut. She pecked him again, this time on the nose.

"Fred, stop that!" Rupert said. "Get back over here."

Fred obeyed and returned to his shoulder. He knelt down beside the body and placed a finger on his pulse. The skin was rough and cold. He was nearing death, but his heart still beat. He rolled the body onto his back and lifted him up in his arms, hoisting him onto the horse.

"Come on, girl. We're going back to Snow Peak. This fellow isn't dying on my watch."

FIVE

ELLA STOOD AT the center of the room. She stared out the window, watching the snow float gently to the ground. She turned her head to see where she was. It was the Snow Peak library. A single, vacant room with shelves lining the walls. Why was she here? She inspected the shelves, but they were all empty. There was only one single book sitting on the center shelf, in the middle of the room.

She grabbed the thick, brick-like book and read the title on the dusty cover; *The Wonderful World of Animals: Volume 5 — Reptiles*. She flipped to a random page. There was a large picture of what appeared to be a turtle. Its skin was dry and flaky. Dirt smudged its enormous shell. There was a short caption below:

Giant Tortoise

There are numerous species and subspecies of the giant tortoise, all spread throughout various parts of the world, but they are typically found in a tropical island setting. Their diet consists of various plants, including grass, flowers, and other greens. As their name suggests, these specimens are very large, weighing as much as 600 pounds and growing up to 4 feet long. Once very prominent around the world, their population has significantly declined. In the days of pirates, many considered tortoise meat a delicacy. Their slow movement made them incredibly easy targets. Tortoise meat is highly resistant to spoiling and has a unique taste. Docked sailors would often capture these creatures in large quantities before setting out on long voyages. Nowadays, giant tortoise sightings are very rare. The giant tortoise can live for over two hundred years.

She stopped reading. *The giant tortoise can live for over two hundred years?* She clapped the pages shut and placed the book back on the shelf before turning around to exit through the front door.

The doorway led to a sandy beach. That's when Ella remembered, Snow Peak was not on top of a snowy mountain range. It was on a tropical island. She shaded her eyes from the sun to get a better view of the shore. The beach was empty, and the waves rolled smoothly over the sand, crashing down just short of her feet. The tide quickly rose, and she soon found herself waist-deep in ocean water. She gently fell back, letting the water hold her up. A strong current swept her floating body away. She shut her eyes and let the cool breeze gently blow across her face.

When she opened her eyes, she was lying in bed. There was a light breeze coming from the window across the room. The air was stinging with frost. She tensed up and bundled her sheets tightly over her shoulders. She glanced out through the window, at the full moon. Outside, there was the silhouette of a slender man. His features were hidden by the darkness of night, as he moved towards the cabin across from hers. "Martha and Patrick," she whispered to herself. The unknown figure entered the cabin. Her eyes stayed fixed on the front door until the figure exited, carrying a body.

She sprung out of bed, but when her bare feet touched the hot sand, she remembered she was not in her bedroom.

She was in the desert, and her bed was not a bed at all, but a giant tortoise. The large desert creature inched forward one foot at a time, leaving a trail of crater-sized footprints. She left the tortoise behind and wandered into the vast fields of sand. She reached the base of a large sand dune and looked up at the towering peak. Bits of sand crumbled from the top as the ground began to shift. The movement grew more violent, knocking Ella off her feet. She fell onto her back and lay still, waiting for the shaking to stop. But it persisted. It grew faster, louder, more intense. It was more than she could handle. Her insides felt like bubbles about to burst. She opened her mouth, ready to scream.

But then she was back in bed. The window across the room was still open, but the full moon was no longer there. It was morning. Ella's mother, Tamara, sat nearby. She shook Ella's shoulder, trying to wake her up. Ella lightly pushed her hand away. "Okay, okay. I'm awake."

Tamara got to her feet. "Get up and get ready Ella. You have work to do. That wood's not going to chop itself, dear."

"Ugh, you don't know that," Ella replied. She peered out the window at Martha and Patrick's cabin. There were no footprints in the snow. No sign of anyone coming or going. "What a crazy dream," she said as she got out of bed.

The giant tortoise can live for over two hundred years.

SIX

V INCE OPENED HIS eyes. His lids scratched against the dry surface of his eyeballs. He blinked rapidly to build moisture, and then squinted as his eyes adjusted to the bright sunlight peeking through the edge of the window curtains. He was lying in a modest bed in the corner of a cozy room. The walls, floor, and ceiling were all made of aged wood panels. The piney aroma filled his nostrils as he took a long deep breath. There was a kitchen in the corner, equipped with a gas stove and a small sink. A blackened fireplace was tucked away in the other corner.

He tried to get up, but a strong pain rang through his body. Arms, shoulders, back, chest, stomach, legs. They all ached. An intense pounding invaded his head with each coming heartbeat. He lay back and tried to gather his thoughts. Where was he? Who had brought him here? Where was Saul?

He rested for a moment and tried to sit up again. He swiveled around and let his legs dangle off the side of the bed. The pain rang through his body again, but this time he ignored it. He carefully slid off the bed and onto his feet. A burning rage devoured his soles, crawling up his legs and clawing at his knees. It was a burn too hot to ignore. He collapsed to the ground, screaming in agony. He lay still while the pain subsided. Once it was gone, he sat upright and folded one leg over the other to inspect his feet. They were heavily bandaged.

He grabbed his ankle and bent it further to get a better look. The bottom of the bandage was a light shade of red. As he removed it, he slowly revealed the gory mess underneath. Bare bone showed in scattered areas, and large chunks of flesh hung from what could barely be called a foot anymore. Most of the bleeding had stopped, but there were still wet spots here and there. He carefully covered the wound back up and patted it lightly.

Examining the room again, he noticed a small metal wheelchair in the corner across from the fireplace. His coat and bag were draped over the back. He crawled on his hands and knees, making his way across the room, and climbed into the chair.

The front door creaked open, and a boy's head poked in. The boy looked no more than seven years old, maybe younger. He slid through the crack and pushed it closed behind him. He stared at Vince. Vince stared back. Neither said a word.

Finally, Vince cleared his throat and quietly introduced himself. "Hello. My name is Vince. What's your name?"

The boy said nothing.

Vince wondered if perhaps the boy did not understand him. Maybe he spoke another language. "Do you understand me?"

Still no answer. The boy just stared blankly at him. Vince had many questions, but clearly this boy was not the one to ask.

"Is there someone in charge? Someone I can speak with?"

The boy smiled and nodded. He opened the door and signaled for Vince to follow. Vince wheeled his chair through the doorway and closed it behind him.

The cold slapped his skin. He reached behind to grab his coat. His aching muscles intensified as he twisted his body. His coat fumbled about in his trembling hands. He draped it over his shoulders and huddled his arms close to his body.

The village was populated with small wooden cabins. A heavy coat of snow covered the roof of each one. The roads were nearly deserted. A lone old man wandered through the snow, spouting nonsense to a non-existent audience. No one else was outside, but faint candlelight glowed from the inside of windows, and dark smoke rose from chimneys in thick puffs. *They must all be inside.* A forest of evergreens bordered the village. The boy stood in the middle of the road, waving his arms over his head to get Vince's attention. When Vince finally looked, the boy signaled for him to follow, entering the cabin across the road.

A beautiful horse stood out in front, tied to a wooden post. Tall and strong with a white hide; its hooves the size of coconuts. Its gorgeous mane fluttered in the light breeze. He took a moment to admire the gentle beast, and then rolled his chair into the road. The thick snow made it difficult. His aching arms burned as he turned the wheels, and his muscles tingled with an unpleasant numbness.

When he reached the other side, he pushed through the door to enter the cabin. The boy was sitting in a chair behind a desk far bigger than he was, swinging his short legs back and forth above the ground. The room was almost identical to the other one. The curtains along the windows. The wooden panels. Even the same piney aroma. He rolled along the hollow sounding floor, and stopped in front of the desk, across from the boy. The wooden chair creaked as the boy kicked his legs and smiled at Vince. Vince smiled back, confused.

"What are we waiting for?" Vince asked.

"Stay here," the boy said finally. He hopped off the chair and left through the back door. When he returned, a large burly man followed closely behind. His massive beard covered his lower face and reached down to his belly. He was well-built with broad shoulders and an imposing posture. The falcon perched on his shoulder glared intensely at Vince.

He walked to the desk and placed a tray in front of Vince. On it was a warm bowl of chili and a cool mug of water. "Eat up. You must be starving," he said with a full jovial voice. "Welcome to Snow Peak. My name is Rupert."

Snow Peak. The name was fitting. Vince had many questions, but the smell of warm food was far too enticing. He took a small sip of water and then shoveled spoonfuls of chili into his mouth. When the bowl was empty, he downed the rest of the water and politely wiped his mouth. "Thank you for your hospitality," he said, "My name is Vince."

"Nice to meet you, Vince. You've already met Carl." He pointed to the boy, who smiled back and waved. "He's a little shy, but his mind's as sharp as a needle. And this here is Fred." He held out his arm and the falcon fluttered over, her eyes still piercing through Vince. "She's one fierce bird."

"She?" Vince said with surprise.

"Yes, Fred is a she." He lowered his voice. "Although, she doesn't know she has a gentleman's name. She is one magnificent bird."

"That's quite a horse you have out there,"

"Yes, it is. Always reliable. Unfortunately, it's the only horse we have.

"Where are we exactly?"

"Like I said, we're in Snow Peak," Rupert said as if the answer was obvious.

"Are there any other towns nearby? I'm not familiar with Snow Peak."

"Sorry friend. Can't help you with that one. We don't have much contact with others. Everything we need is right here."

"You don't have contact with others?"

"Nope. Just you and Fred. Occasionally, traders come through, but they never stay too long."

"You haven't seen a man pass through recently, have you? Skinny, black hat?

Rupert paused, lost in deep thought. "There was that one fellow out in the snow plains. I saw him right around the same time I found you. I didn't get a good look at him, but I do recall a black hat. But he never came through town. He turned towards the forest. I considered following him, but you were in bad shape. You needed to be treated right away. It's a miracle you're even alive right now."

"How long was I out?"

"We found you two days ago. We were all pretty worried. I've never seen that much blood before." He glanced at Vince's feet. "You look okay now, though."

"Do you know where that forest leads? Where is he headed?"

"I go into the woods to hunt, but I stay fairly close by. I don't know what else is out there, other than trees."

"Saul," Vince whispered to himself. "What are you up to?"

"What was that?" Rupert leaned forward, turning his ears.

Vince almost repeated Saul's name but decided against it. They did not need to know about Saul. Not yet. "Nothing. Just thinking out loud."

"I hope—"

An older lady burst through the door, interrupting his thought. Panic lingered in her eyes. She leaned against the wall, out of breath. "Rupe…Rupe…" She tried to speak, but her panting was too rapid. She took a short moment until finally the words spilled from her mouth. "Rupert! Another person is missing!"

Frustration swept across Rupert's face. "Damn it!" He yelled, startling Vince. Just seconds earlier, the man was both kind and welcoming. Even Fred was a little startled by his outburst. He took a moment to calm himself and turned to the lady. "Who's missing?" he asked in an aggressively calm tone.

She began to tear up. "Patrick," she answered.

Rupert released a long tired sigh. "Is Martha okay?"

"She's upset, but she's safe."

"Good." He stood up. "I'll take a look at their cabin. See if I can find anything helpful. I just hope we have better luck than we did with Alan's cabin. Can Martha stay with you until we have this sorted out?

"Of course."

"Thank you, Mary. Carl, go with her." Carl ran over to Mary, and they left the room. Rupert glanced back at Vince. "Make yourself at home. I'll be back as soon as I can."

"Can I come with you?"

Rupert furrowed his brow. "If you really want to, I don't see why not."

He walked behind the wheelchair to push, but Vince waved him off. He wanted to do it himself.

SEVEN

VINCE FOLLOWED RUPERT back out into the cold. Pushing the chair through the snow was much easier now. A little food and water went a long way.

The old man was still outside, and just as nonsensical as before. Rupert caught Vince staring at him. "Don't mind him. His mind isn't what it used to be, but he means well. He has some good days, some bad. It looks like today is one of the bad ones. He'll be fine, though. Come on, let's get moving."

As they approached the cabin, Rupert saw Mary, Martha, and Carl through the window next door. Martha was sobbing, and Mary and Carl tried desperately to comfort her. There was only one set of footprints, leading from Martha's cabin to Mary's. "Those must be Martha's footprints."

"There are no others?" Vince asked. "How did he leave without leaving footprints?"

Rupert had no answer.

"Did it snow last night?" Vince asked. "Maybe the snow covered them up."

"No. It was a clear sky last night."

"Hmm."

Before entering, Rupert circled the perimeter but found nothing of interest.

The room inside was also almost identical to the others. The only difference was a slightly bigger bed. The room itself was in perfect condition. Nothing unusual. No signs of a disturbance.

"It's like no one was ever here," Vince said, amazed. "The room looks untouched."

Rupert nodded. "Just like yesterday."

"Yesterday?"

"One of our others, Alan, went missing two nights ago. I checked his cabin yesterday. It was exactly like this. No footprints. No struggle. Like no one was ever there."

"Did anyone see anything?" Vince had his suspicions about these kidnappings, but he was not yet ready to share. He wanted to learn more first.

"No one saw anything. Not even Alan's wife. She slept through the night. I suspect it will be the same with Martha. It's like they just vanished into thin air."

When they were done inspecting the room, they went next door to speak with Martha. When they arrived, Carl had left, but the two women remained. Martha was no longer crying.

"Where's Carl?" Rupert asked.

Mary looked up, surprised that they were already done. "He's getting food for Martha. Did you find anything?"

"Nothing. Just like with Alan. There are no footprints and everything looks normal." He glanced at Martha. "Did you hear or see anything last night. Anything at all."

She shook her head. "No. We went to sleep, and when I woke up, he was gone."

"Nothing unusual happened last night?" Vince asked.

"I'm sorry, who are you?"

Rupert patted him on the shoulder. "This is Vince. He's the one I found up in the mountains a few days ago."

Vince leaned forward to shake her hand. "I'm sorry for your loss."

"Please don't say that." More tears ran down her cheeks. "You make it sound like he's dead."

"I'm sorry. That was not my intention."

Carl came back holding a bowl of chili.

Rupert gently rubbed Martha's back. "You go ahead and eat. I think we know everything that there is to know right now. I'll call a town meeting later today. People should know what's going on." Rupert left, and Vince followed.

Martha held the bowl of chili but didn't eat. Instead, she just stared at it.

EIGHT

ELLA SLAMMED HER ax down on the log, watching it split cleanly down the middle. Chopping wood was exhausting, but she did it so often it was second nature. Just another of the many chores she took over when her father passed away.

She stood over the pile of wood, satisfied with her work, when her mother called from the back porch. "Ella, could you run out to the library? I need a few things."

"Of course, Mother." She wedged the ax into the chopping block and headed inside. Her mother provided a list of three books: a recipe book for stews, a guide to edible plants, and a book about herbs and spices. Her mother had recently developed an interest in cooking and was experimenting with new dishes. Ella found herself making trips to the library more often these days, but she did not mind. She enjoyed browsing the shelves and discovering new books.

On her walk over, she came across the old man in his usual spot, yelling and stomping his feet in the snow. Ella approached him with a smile. "Hello, Horace," she said in her most cheery voice. "You're looking handsome today." Horace quieted down and attempted a lopsided smile. Ella chuckled "Okay honey, don't outdo yourself with all that yelling. Wouldn't want you to lose your voice." She patted his shoulder. "See you later."

When she arrived at the library, it was completely empty. Not unusual for this time of day. She pulled out her mother's list. First, a recipe book for stews. She browsed the shelves. *The Secrets to Home Cooking: Soups and Stews.* Perfect. She adored soups. Perhaps she could convince her mother to brew a nice hot batch of corn chowder.

Second, a guide to edible plants. For this, she picked out *Knowing Your Greens: How to Find Delicious Plants and Avoid the Dangerous Ones.*

To finish off the list, a book about herbs and spices. There were many books of the sort. Endless options to choose from. After a few minutes of searching, she picked up *Spice Up Your Life: Herbs and Spices That Will Change the*

Way You Cook. Spice books were all the same, but this one had a fun cover.

With the last book in her bag, she headed towards the exit but stopped just short of the door. She turned around and slowly walked to the center shelf in the middle of the room. The book was in exactly the spot she knew it would be. She pulled it off the shelf and ran her fingers over the cover. *The Wonderful World of Animals: Volume 5 — Reptiles.*

She cracked open the cover and skipped directly to the index sliding her finger down the page, searching for G. When she found it, she eagerly flipped to the page and stared at the words:

Giant Tortoise

There are numerous species and subspecies of the giant tortoise, all spread throughout various parts of the world, but they are typically found in a tropical island setting. Their diet consists of various plants, including grass, flowers, and other greens. As their name suggests, these specimens are very large, weighing as much as 600 pounds, and growing up to 4 feet long. Once very prominent around the world, their population has significantly declined. In the days of pirates, many considered tortoise meat a delicacy. Their slow movement made them incredibly easy targets.

Tortoise meat is highly resistant to spoiling and has a unique taste. Docked sailors would often capture these creatures in large quantities before setting out on long voyages. Nowadays, giant tortoise sightings are very rare. The giant tortoise can live for over two hundred years.

Again, this last sentence lingered in her mind. *The giant tortoise can live for over two hundred years.* Why did this fascinate her so much?

A bell rang from outside, and a man walked past the window. "Attention everyone! There will be a town meeting held this evening in the auditorium! Attendance is mandatory! I repeat! Attendance is mandatory!" The announcement faded as the man carried the message along. Ella stuffed *The Wonderful World of Animals* in her bag, along with the other books, and headed out the door.

NINE

T HE AUDITORIUM WAS completely full. The seats were packed, and groups of people stood along the walls. Vince arrived early with Rupert and made his way up to the front row. His feet were better, if only slightly. There was still a stinging pain that would last for a while.

In front of the audience was a small elevated stage with a tall podium. Casual conversation rumbled through the room as people waited for the meeting to start.

The crowd died down as Rupert, with Fred perched on his shoulder, approached the podium. He placed both palms down on the wood surface and cleared his throat. "Good evening, everyone. Thank you for coming to this meeting. I know these have been frequent, but this is important. I'm afraid I have some bad news. As you all know, Alan went missing yesterday morning." People in the crowd nodded. "Well, I'm afraid it has happened again. This afternoon we discovered that Patrick is missing as well."

A collective gasp filled the room, followed by panic. They rose up in a concerned uproar, all asking the same questions to different people. What does this mean? Will this happen again? Who will be next?

"Everyone!" Rupert yelled, "Please quiet down!" No one could hear him over the shouts of fear and frustration. Fred hopped onto the podium. She spread her wings out wide, opened her beak, and released a tremendous shriek. The chaos stopped in an instant. They all turned and looked to Rupert.

"Thank you, girl." The obedient falcon returned to her spot on his shoulder. "Now, obviously, this is a tragedy. We must support Martha in her time of need. That goes without saying. However, we must also prepare for the future. With Alan and Patrick's disappearance, I see a pattern forming. I can only assume that the same thing will happen tonight. We must ensure that everyone is safe in their beds. I propose a night watch. A team of people that can patrol the roads. We are going to need volunteers. Ten people. Two shifts of five. Fred and I will take the northeast corner for the first shift. Is anyone else interested? Please stand."

A few whispers roamed the crowd. Fourteen people stood. Seven men, six women, and a little girl.

Rupert smiled at the child. "Thank you, darling. You are very brave, but I would feel better with you safe inside your home tonight." She sat back down. "The rest of you, come see me once we're done here. We can sort out the details and assign shifts." The rest of them sat down as well. "Next, we must gather a search party. There is already a group searching for Alan, but I'd like to double our efforts. I will lead this new group. We will leave in the morning at eight o'clock. Volunteers?"

Five people stood, some of them the same as before.

"Thank you, especially to those who volunteered twice. However, I think it is important that the search party is well-rested, so I ask that nobody participates in both. Again, see me after the meeting and we can sort out the details. Lastly, I am trying to gather as much information as I can. I know it's unlikely, but did anyone see anything out of the ordin…?"

The doors in the back burst open, and a screaming Horace stumbled in. He spouted out his usual gibberish.

Rupert stepped down from the podium and spoke softly to two men in the front row. They both stood up and escorted Horace out. Rupert returned to the podium.

"Sorry about that. They will make sure Horace gets home safely. Now, where was I? Oh right. Did anyone see anything strange last night?"

A hand popped up near the back of the room. A red haired girl in her early twenties rose from her seat and spoke in a full voice. "I saw something."

Rumbles in the crowd started building up again. "Okay everybody," Rupert said. "Let the girl talk. Go ahead Ella."

"As you all know, I live across from Martha and Patrick. I have a clear view of their cabin from my window. Last night, I awoke and saw a figure. It was too dark to see from a distance, but the figure was tall and slender. I could tell that much. He entered their cabin, and when he came back out, he was carrying a body." She slowly dropped her head with sorrow, and then raised it up again. "I thought it was just a dream, so I didn't think much of it, but now I know it was real. Dreams are never so vivid."

"Thank you, Ella. I will speak with you later. Did anyone else see anything? It is extremely important that we have as much information as possible" There was no response. "If you do see anything, don't hesitate to come find me. That concludes our meeting. You're free to go. Volunteers come see me."

The crowd cleared out. Rupert informed the volunteers and sent them home to rest before their shift.

He then turned to Ella. "I hope you don't mind helping us."

"Not at all. I want to help."

"Your mother doesn't mind?

"Don't worry about her. She'll be fine."

"Good. To tell you the truth, we really have no information. There was nothing in either of the cabins. No footprints. Nothing. It looked like they just vaporized. But you can confirm that's not true. They were taken, or at least Patrick was. I assume the same thing happened to Alan."

Vince watched as Rupert and Ella discussed the details of the kidnapping or lack thereof. Neither of them had a clue what they were up against, but Vince did. People were beginning to panic, and the lack of answers only made things worse. He decided it was time they knew what he did. "Rupert, I have something important to tell you."

Ella looked down at Vince. "I don't think we've met. I'm Ella."

He reached up and firmly shook her hand. "I'm Vince. Nice to meet you."

"This is the man I found in the mountains," Rupert said.

A look of excitement jumped across her face. "Oh yeah! The lucky survivor. You're recovering well. From what I hear, you were in pretty bad condition."

"Yes, I'm feeling much better. Thank you."

"So what is it?" Rupert asked. "What do you want to tell me?"

"I know who's kidnapping your people. His name is Saul. He is a very dangerous man." Vince paused. "It's quite a long story. Let's go back to your cabin, and I'll tell you from the beginning."

They returned to Rupert's cabin and dished out bowls of chili. Gathered around the fireplace, Vince began his story.

TEN

Many years ago…

THE WOODS NEAR Rodin were gorgeous. A hidden paradise. The sunlight peeked through the branches, creating a collage of light and shadow on the ground. Critters scurried about. Squirrels, rabbits, chipmunks, birds. The woods were teeming with life.

Two boys, both twelve years old, stood on the branches of a tall tree. They raced to the top, hopping from one to another. One of the boys pushed off with his feet and soared through the air, arms extended forward. He stretched the tips of his fingers, ready to grab the next branch, but missed and plunged to the ground. He rolled onto his back and looked up with embarrassment. The other boy carefully stepped up to touch the top branch. He raised his arms up in the air to celebrate his victory. Vince had won the race.

They both heard a distant voice, "Vincent! Saul! Time to come in! Dinner's ready!"

"Okay, Mother!" Vince yelled from the top of the tree. "We'll be right there!" He climbed down and helped Saul to his feet. "Looks like I win again."

"One of these days you'll be the one lying on the ground."

"Right, Saul. You keep saying that."

"I say it because it's true. You'll see. One of these days."

They walked towards Vince's house, playfully pushing each other along the way. When they reached the top of the hill, Saul turned to look back at the woods. His eyes swept across the forest, a place where he and Vince could relax and have fun after school. In a shadowy crevice beneath a tree, a man stood, staring at them. He was tall and slender and wore a fitted black suit. Saul glanced at Vince, and then back to the woods, but the man was gone.

"Did you see that?" Saul yelled over to Vince, who was already making his way down the other side of the hill.

Vince turned around. "See what?"

"There was a man in the woods…just staring at us. And then he vanished. Come on, let's go check it out." He stepped back towards the woods.

"Saul, wait! My mother is waiting for us. We can't just leave her."

"Don't you want to know who is watching us?"

"We can check it out tomorrow, but right now we need to go home."

Saul swept his eyes across the woods once more.

"Come on Saul, my mother is going to get upset."

"Fine, let's go. I'm starving anyway."

When they got to Vince's house, his mother was waiting for them at the door. "Come on, boys. Clean up and set the table." They did as she said.

With the table set, they sat down and joined Vince's parents. His father placed a big bowl of stew in front of them. "Eat up. You boys must be hungry after all of that messing around."

Vince inhaled the scent of slow-cooked beef rising up from the bowl. His stomach grumbled and his mouth filled with saliva. He grabbed his spoon and dug into the food. Saul did the same.

"Easy there," his father said. "Eat like that and you'll choke on your food."

"Leave them alone," his mother said. "They're growing boys. They need to fatten up."

"Don't get too fat. You're getting older, son. Soon you'll be helping me out a lot more with the shop. I'll take you out hunting, but you have to be in shape to keep up with me out there."

Vince slowed his eating when his father mentioned hunting. It was something he had wanted to do for a long time. Go out to the woods and bring in the meat. Contribute to the family business. His father was right. He should stay in shape. He put down his spoon, leaving his bowl half full.

"Don't listen to your father. He'll take you out hunting no matter what. He's just being a grouch."

He shrugged and laughed. "Well, someone has to be grouchy around here. Everyone's always so cheery."

Vince looked at his mother, then at his father, and started shoveling the second half of the food into his mouth.

After dinner, the boys helped clean the dishes and then Saul left for home. Vince was exhausted as he got ready for bed. He lay down and placed his head on the soft pillow, quickly shutting his eyes and entering a deep slumber.

*****

A soft tapping noise woke Vince up. He looked around and saw Saul standing outside the window. He got out of bed and cracked the window open. "Saul, what are you doing here?"

"I can't sleep."

"So you came here?"

"Yeah. I'm going to find that man in the woods."

"Can't it wait until morning?"

Saul shook his head. "We have school in the morning. He'll be long gone by the time we get out of school. We're both awake right now, so let's just go."

"I'm awake because you woke me up," Vince muttered. "Why do you need me anyway? Go on your own."

"I want someone with me, in case something happens. I promise we'll be back before sunrise. Your parents won't even know you were gone."

Vince looked into his eyes and saw he was determined to find this man. He would go whether Vince came or not. If something bad *did* happen, he would never forgive himself. Also, he was almost certain that this man was just a figment of Saul's imagination. It was best for him to keep an eye on Saul, to make sure he did not get into any real trouble. "Okay, I'll come. Just give me a minute." He changed out of his pajamas and into warmer clothes. Saul helped him through the window, and they walked back towards the woods.

As they walked, Vince pulled out two hunting knives. "I brought these." He unsheathed one of them and examined the blade. It was dull, but it would have to do. He clipped one to the side of his belt and handed the other to Saul. "If anything happens, we'll be ready."

Saul held the blade up in the moonlight, admiring its metal glow. He had never held a hunting knife before. "Where did you get these?"

"They belong to my father. He uses them to hunt. These ones are old."

They approached the woods and Saul pointed. "That's where I saw him. Right there."

"Right here?"

Saul nodded.

"I don't see anything. No sign that anyone was here."

"Do you see tracks or anything like that? Something we could follow?"

Vince briefly looked around. It was dark, but his eyes had adjusted. "I don't see anything. What did you say he looked like?"

"I didn't get a good look, but he was tall and skinny. He wore a tight black suit."

"What kind of suit?"

"I don't know. I've never seen anyone wear clothes like that before. He looked strange."

"So what do you want to do? We have no leads, no trail to follow."

Saul threw his arms in the air, both disappointed and frustrated. "Do you think I'm lying, Vince? I know what I saw. There was a man in a suit standing here, watching us."

"I don't think you're lying. I just find it a little hard to believe. Maybe you were imagining things."

"I was not imagining things." Saul pointed deeper into the woods. "I saw him go that way. Let's keep walking. Maybe we'll find something out there."

Vince did not argue. He was not in the mood to argue. This was something Saul needed to get out of his system, and then they could go home. As they trudged deeper into the woods, Vince peered up at the tall trees. The branches and leaves were growing thicker as they walked. The moonlight faded with each step they took. And then he noticed a small rectangular box perched high up in the branches. It looked like metal and had a round stubby piece on the front. He pointed up. "What is that?"

Saul followed his finger up the tree and saw the strange box. "I don't know."

Vince scratched his head. "It's not part of the tree. It's made of metal or something. Someone must have put it up there."

"How would anyone get up there? That tree's impossible to climb."

Saul was right. The tree was ten times taller than the one they were climbing earlier, and the stepping branches were scarce. There was no way anyone could get up there.

"I don't know but…Wait! Did it just move?"

Saul looked at Vince. "Move? It's a hundred feet up in the air. How would it move?"

"I saw it move."

"You're just tired. You're seeing things."

Vince strained his eyes, waiting for it to move again, but it did not. "You're right. I *am* tired. And do you know why? Because you woke me up in the middle of the night to go searching for an imaginary man in a suit. I let you have your fun, but let's face it, we're not going to find anyone out here. Can we just go home?"

"Soon, I promise. Just give me a few more minutes."

As they continued further into the woods, Saul frantically turned his head, looking for any signs that the man in the suit existed. Vince followed closely behind, observing Saul, rather than their surroundings. After several minutes with more of the same, they both stopped to rest, sitting on a nearby log. They stared into the darkness as an ominous silence washed over, and a thick cloud of fog rolled in. Chills crawled over Vince's skin, and Saul was visibly trembling.

"I give up," Saul muttered. "Let's go home."

"Finally!" Vince stood up, but quickly realized the fog had grown thick. They would get lost if they wandered off now. Saul was only a few feet away, but he could barely see him at all. He sat back down. "Let's wait for the fog to pass."

Saul's face was a mess. He turned to Vince. "This was a mistake. We never should have come out here."

Vince looked back with disdain "You're the one who dragged me out here in the first place. I could be lying comfortably in my bed right now."

"Don't blame me for being here. I didn't force you to come. If you had said no, I would have left you alone."

"And then you would be stranded out here by yourself, hunting down some mystery man. Who knows what could have happened to you? You should be thanking me." Saul's lack of gratitude was getting under Vince's skin.

"Look, I don't want to argue right now. Let's just both shut up and wait for the fog to pass."

They waited, but the fog did not pass.

ELEVEN

THE FIREPLACE CRACKLED, its warmth filling the air. Rupert, Fred, and Ella all huddled around Vince as he told his story. They had so many questions. Who was this man in the suit? Why was Saul so dangerous? But before he could answer these questions, his story was interrupted by the sound of screaming from outside. Rupert looked at the others curiously and got to his feet.

When he opened the door, a crowd of people ran by, holding torches and shouting. Vince and Ella followed Rupert outside. They stood in the road while people passed by. Ella stopped one of them. "What's happening? Where is everyone going?"

"Someone's coming out of the woods. It's got to be that monster, here to take someone else. We have to stop him. Come on, this way." The man ran off. Rupert and Ella followed.

"No, wait," Vince hollered. "He'll kill you all!"

But no one heard his yells. He pushed the wheels of his chair, but the thick snow and steep incline made it impossible to keep up. His arms cramped as he groaned in frustration. He could not let another town vanish. He could not let Saul win again. He jumped to his feet, but the burning pain was too much. He dropped to the ground and squirmed helplessly on the ground. There was no way he could stop Saul. Not like this.

Behind him, he heard the dampened clop of large hooves in the snow. Rupert's horse was still tied to the post in front of the cabin. Vince could ride it over to the others. He crawled over to the majestic beast, but there was no way for him to mount the thing from the ground. He could barely even stand. He looked into the creature's gloomy face. "Sorry buddy, but I have to do this." He pressed both hands into the horse's warm stomach and closed his eyes.

The creature turned from calm to agitated, shaking about with discomfort. Its white hide withered to a fiery crimson. Agitation turned to anger as it wildly kicked in all directions. Vince dodged the powerful blows, keeping his hands glued to the delirious animal. The horse jumped and threw its hind legs in the air, groaning loudly. Its amber hide darkened to a deep black. Its energy depleted as it slowed its kicks and finally stopped. It stumbled and fell to its knees. Vince moved his hands up to the creature's back. It sat in the snow, wheezing and exhausted. It let out a final cry of agony and collapsed into a lifeless corpse. Its black hide faded to a pale gray.

Adrenaline coursed through Vince's veins. He stood up with ease and dug his feet into the snow. No more pain. No more exhaustion. He felt unstoppable.

Carl was standing behind him, stiff as a board, eyes wide open. His whole body shook as Vince walked over. "Sorry you had to see that. I'm afraid I don't have time to explain right now." He walked past Carl and sprinted towards the woods. Hopefully, everyone was not already dead.

Carl stared at the corpse of Rupert's horse, confused and frightened.

TWELVE

THE CROWD WAS gathered just outside of the woods. Vince slowed to a casual walk when he saw everyone was safe. They were gathered in a tight circle, and a steady chatter of whispers filled the silence. "What's happening?" he asked. "Where is Saul?"

The lady in front of him turned around, startled. "Saul? Who's Saul? Is that the person who came out of the woods? I can't see from back here."

Vince agreed. He needed to get closer. He circled around, but couldn't get a good view. He could hear Rupert's muffled voice, coming from the center of the group. He weaved his way through, cutting between people until he saw Rupert.

Rupert stood with a man, shaking his hand and patting his back. The man's face held a wide grin. A woman broke through the crowd, passed by Vince, and flung herself into the man's arms. She kissed him, tears pouring down her face. Rupert's smile grew larger when he noticed Vince among the crowd. "Vince…you're walking! And you look terrific. This is truly a miraculous night. Come here, I want you to meet someone. This is Alan."

Vince stuck his hand out. Alan grabbed it and shook with enthusiasm. "Good to meet you, Vince."

"Alan," Rupert said. "You've been through a lot. We can talk about what happened to you in the morning, but for now, you should spend the night with your wife." He turned to the crowd. "Our good friend Alan has returned!" A cheer rang through the people. "We will rejoice tomorrow, but for now, we let him rest. Of course, those who are volunteering, please continue your shift. It is much appreciated."

The crowd dispersed, and the people returned to their cabins. Alan went home with his overjoyed wife. Rupert, Ella, and Vince walked back together.

"You're walking!" Ella said. "And you look great!"

"I feel great. Much better than I have in some time." He looked back to the cabin Alan had retired to. "Who is that man, anyway?"

"Alan was the first to go missing," Rupert answered, "two nights ago, before Patrick. If Alan returned, maybe Patrick will too. We're not going to stop looking, that's for sure. We'll learn more about what happened tomorrow morning when we talk to him. I'm excited. We finally have something more than just speculation to help us."

They walked in silence for a moment, and then Rupert asked, "Vince, how are you walking? I wrapped up your feet no more than a day ago. They were torn to shreds. How is that possible?"

Vince knew they would ask, but he had no idea how to respond. No explanation. Would they even believe him if he told the truth? Before Vince could answer, Ella shrieked with terror. Fred followed up with a frightened screech.

"Good lord!" Rupert exclaimed. They stood over the dead corpse of Rupert's horse. Carl, who had not moved, turned around to face the four of them. Rupert knelt down, meeting the boy's eyes. "Carl, what happened here?"

Carl lifted his finger and pointed at Vince. They all glared with horrified disbelief.

Rupert looked sternly into Vince's eyes. "You've got some explaining to do, stranger."

Vince brought them inside and continued his story.

THIRTEEN

THE BOYS SAT on the log, waiting for the fog to pass, but it did not. It remained thick and grew even steadier. Vince grew restless with every passing minute, irritated at Saul for dragging him out of his house in the middle of the night.

They both stared into the white sheet that had enveloped them. "What do you think is out there?" Vince asked.

"I already told you what I saw. A man wearing a suit."

"No. I mean what do you think is *out there*? You know, beyond the border. Outside of the Pugg."

Saul had no answer. He had never left Rodin, let alone the Pugg. "I don't know. You've been out of town more than I have. Weren't you in Pifftyn a while ago?"

"Yeah, it's a dump. You're not missing much."

"It can't be worse than Rodin, can it?"

Vince kicked a pebble near his feet. "Rodin isn't so bad. Sure, it's no Vassor, but you can't expect it to be."

"You've been to Vassor?" Saul asked, surprised.

"A while back. A few years ago. My father brought me to help sell meat. We barely got any business."

"What was it like? Was it nice?"

"Yeah. The houses were huge, and the roads were so clean you could eat off of them. Men wore suits that shined with silver. Women were covered from head to toe in jewelry."

"Amazing! Imagine what it would be like to live in such a place."

"No point in thinking about it," Vince said. "There's no way we can ever afford to live there. I didn't really like it anyway. The locals looked down on us. Like they were better than us."

"Well, they have reason to act like that. They are the wealthiest town in the Pugg."

Saul was right. Vassor was the heart of the Pugg. It held all of the big stores, all of the important people. When Vince went with his father, they spent the whole day admiring the tall stone buildings, and the majestic horses around every corner. He was impressed and amazed at first, but when he returned home, he realized just how repulsive the people were.

"I've never met anyone from Vassor," Saul continued, "but all I know is, the second I can afford to live there, I'm gone."

"Believe me, it was way too fancy for you. The place is crowded, too. You wouldn't like it. There *was* one place I liked there. It was tucked behind the lawmen horse stables. Right next to a strange looking tree. You should have seen this tree. Its trunk was split down the middle three ways, almost symmetrically. I had never seen anything like it. It looked like the tentacles of those deep sea creatures we read about in the books." He glanced at Saul and could tell he did not care much about the tree. "Anyway, there was a cave hidden next to the tree, behind some hanging moss. Nobody else knew it was there. It was a quiet place I liked to hide in, to get away from the people. It reminded me of the woods here in Rodin. Peaceful."

"Let me get this right. You go to the biggest, most luxurious place in the Pugg, a place that people would kill for just to see…and you stay in a cave?" Saul shuffled back and forth, baffled. "That doesn't make sense."

"You would understand if you met the people."

A man clumsily leaped from the bushes, almost falling over, but catching himself at the last minute. He wore a suit, fitting Saul's description, unlike any outfit they had seen before. It was extravagant, but also a bit short for the man wearing it. His lanky arms stuck out far beyond his sleeves, and the bottom of his pants stopped short of his ankles. He had a slender figure, and his short hair was a tangled mess. The strap of his bulky bag stretched over his shoulder and across his chest. Overall, he looked odd.

The man adjusted his posture, clasped his hands together, stuck out his chest, cleared his throat, and began his jovial presentation. "Hello hello hello, gentlemen!" he announced with an animated voice. "I apologize if I stumble over my words. I am not accustomed to making such speeches to fine gentlemen like yourselves, but alas I must. So here we go." Vince and Saul exchanged looks, both surprised and confused. His accent was foreign. He spoke with the speed and energy of a salesman. "I have an offer for you gentlemen today. A very special offer. Something you have never seen before. An opportunity that will never come again. Just one simple word…immortality." He paused for dramatic effect. "Yes, that's right. You heard me correctly. I offer you the power to live forever if you so desire."

"I think we should go," Vince said nervously. He tugged on Saul's shirt. "Come on." They started to back away.

"Wait! Don't go," the man pleaded. "I understand your skepticism, but please just hear what I have to say." His voice jumped up to a desperate tone. "I can't mess up my first presentation. Greene would be furious. Give me five minutes. Then I promise I'll let you go."

The desperation in the man's voice was genuine, and the boys were curious about his intriguing offer. They kept their distance but let him continue.

"Thank you. I promise you will not regret it." He paused again, to gather his thoughts. His lips moved quickly as he mumbled to himself, trying to find where he left off. "Okay. So, immortality." He reached into his bag and pulled out two tubes filled with liquid. "These contain the secret to eternal life. Now you may ask, 'How is this possible? What is this strange concoction he offers us?' And to that, I say, it is a concoction that will change your life forever, in the most literal sense." He pulled a device from his bag. It was a long metal rod with a needle sticking out from the bottom. He loaded one of the tubes into a slot on top. "This is a compound designed to alter your body. Just one small injection and in moments you will gain access to life everlasting." With these words, he cocked his chin up and spread his arms above his head. "I can already see your questions. 'How does this work? How will I live forever?' and the answer is quite simple. Once you take the injection, you will have the amazing ability to drain the energy of life."

"Drain life?" Vince interrupted. "You mean kill?"

"Technically, yes. Whatever you drain will die. However, think about it like this. You hunt and kill for food, right? You already kill animals to stay alive. Draining is no different. It works on plants, too. On trees. These woods are overflowing with energy right now. You'll feel younger. Stronger. This is the end of age as you know it. Just think of the possibilities. You could live forever."

Vince looked to the horizon and saw the orange sun rising. Rays of light peeked through the trees and scared away the darkness. The fog had completely passed, and the woods were now clear. "Saul, the sun's coming up. We have to get home." He turned to the man. "Sorry, we're not interested."

"I understand your hesitation. I am a stranger after all, but I assure you, this product is completely safe. I do not wish to harm you. I only wish to help."

"Thank you for your presentation," Vince said, "but again, we must respectfully decline." He pulled on Saul's arm.

"No, please!" the man pleaded. "You mustn't leave. I *need* you to take these injections." He had dropped to his knees. "Please! Greene will not be happy if this transaction fails. I can't mess this up."

The boys stood and watched as the man fell apart.

"You must accept my offer. It's the only way." He got to his feet and stepped towards them, the loaded needle in his hand.

Vince clenched the knife from his belt. "Stay back. Don't come any closer. We gave you your chance. We listened to what you had to say. Now let us leave."

Saul found himself standing between the two. He stared at the man with nervous anticipation, and carefully backed away toward Vince.

Silence fell upon the woods. The man halted, staring at them with conflicted desperation. Vince backed away, one hand around Saul's arm, the other still gripping his knife. He kept his eyes locked on the man as he inched back. The boys took one step. Then another. And another. And *bump*…Vince's heel caught a root, sending him tumbling over. He twisted around and hit the ground, face first. In a daze, he rubbed the dirt from his cheek, when he heard Saul cry out in pain. He hopped to his feet and turned around. The man stood crouched over Saul. The needle he held was now empty. Saul was on his back, frozen with fear. A red mark swelled on his arm.

Vince marched forward and pulled out his knife. "Get away from him!" He raised the blade over his head and brought it down with all his strength. The dull metal pierced through the skin and sliced through the jellies of his eyeball. When Vince pulled it loose, blood and juice spurted out.

The man dropped to his knees and clasped his face, screaming in agony. "My eye! You cut my eye!"

Vince pulled Saul up from the ground. "Come on," he said. "Let's get out of here." They turned their backs to the blood-soaked man and sprinted away. The painful screams grew faint in the distance until they were completely gone.

The sun continued to rise. The morning birds awakened, filling the tranquil woods with their songs. The boys kept their pace somewhere between a walk and a jog. Perhaps it was the adrenaline pumping through their blood, or the dazed confusion of the whole situation, but the trip back felt shorter than they remembered.

When they reached the edge of the woods, the sun had fully risen. They returned to Vince's house. He climbed through his window and whispered to Saul, "How are you feeling?" He glanced at the mark on his arm. The swelling was worse, and the redness was brighter. "Are you okay?"

Saul nodded, gently rubbing the mark. "I'll be fine."

"Good. I'll see you at school then." He closed the window and jumped into bed. Hoping for just a little rest before school, he shut his eyes and began to doze off.

Knock! Knock! His father burst through the door with loads of energy. "Rise and shine, kid. It's a beautiful day. Hurry up. You're going to be late."

Vince slumped out of bed, ready to face the day, completely exhausted.

FOURTEEN

THE BOYS WANDERED into school like mindless zombies, arms swinging from side to side. The whole class, including the teacher, noticed their pale skin and vacant eyes as they took their seats in the third row. "What happened to you guys?" said a voice from behind. "Did you get beat up or something?"

They turned around to see the boy sitting behind them. Long locks of curly brown hair dangled in front of his face, hiding his dark eyes. He wore a shirt slightly too tight for a boy so chubby. "Excuse me?" Vince said. "Who are you?"

Before the boy could answer, Ms. Martin started class. "Good morning class. Now that everyone is here," she glanced at Vince and Saul as if to point them out, "I can introduce our new student. Roger, please come up here with me." The chubby boy stood up and made his way towards the front of the room. He stood at Ms. Martin's side and turned around to face the class. "This is Roger," she continued as she placed a hand on his shoulder. "He and his family just moved into town. I want you all to make sure he feels welcome. Why don't you tell us a little about yourself, Roger? Where are you from? What kind of things do you like?"

"It would be my pleasure, Ms. Martin." He joined his hands together and excessively cleared his throat. "My name is Roger. I moved here from Vassor."

"Vassor?" Saul whispered to Vince. "He must be one spoiled kid."

Vince hushed him.

"I enjoy reading and school. And of course, nice teachers." He flashed a quick smile at Ms. Martin, who blushed and smiled back. Saul rolled his eyes. "I especially enjoy hanging out with kids who can't defend themselves." He flashed an identical smile at Saul, this time to mock, not flatter.

"Is this guy serious?" Saul muttered to Vince as the rest of the class chuckled at the uninspired insult. "Is this what people in Vassor are like? You were right. He's obnoxious."

"Relax, Saul," Vince said. "He's just messing with you. It's just a joke."

"Okay Roger," Ms. Martin said as the laughs finally stopped. "Enough of that. We don't tolerate that kind of behavior, but it's your first day. I'll excuse it just this once. Don't let it happen again. Now please, return to your seat." He walked back, nudging Saul along the way. Saul tensed up. He wanted to punch the new kid, but he managed to stop himself.

Before Ms. Martin could continue with her schedule for the day, Vince raised his hand. "Ms. Martin, I have a question."

"Go ahead, Vincent."

"I was thinking about it last night. What's outside of the Pugg? What is the rest of the world like?"

"That is a very good question. One that I do not have an answer to. I'm afraid no one knows what lies beyond the Pugg's four towns. There are a handful of curious people who have journeyed across the flatlands, but none ever returned. I'm sure some of you have heard of Harry Hedcrown, one of the Pugg's top innovators, born right here in Rodin. He planned such a journey off to the east. He told the people that if he found something, anything at all, he would return to report it, but we never saw him again. So, as far as we know, there is absolutely nothing out there… Does that answer your question, Vincent?"

Vince nodded.

"Good. Now let's get along with the class. We have a lot to cover."

The class was like any other, bland and uninteresting. Vince was one of the top students in the group, but a night with no sleep made it hard to focus. Saul slouched in his seat, eyes drooping as drowsiness pulled him deeper. But then he sat up, fully alert in an instant. Like a switch, he had gone from zombie to living. He squirmed in his seat with anxiety, tapping his foot rapidly against his desk. Where had all of this energy come from? For the rest of the class, Vince ignored Ms. Martin and kept his focus on Saul.

When class was finally over, the boys met outside. Before Vince could say a word, Saul grabbed him by the shoulders. "It works."

"What?"

"The stuff that man gave me. It actually works." A big smile was plastered across his face.

"Are you sure? How is that even possible?"

"I don't know. I didn't notice much difference at first. Just the rash on my arm. But in the middle of class, it kicked in." His eyes were wide open. "Vince…I can feel the energy. It's all around us. I can feel it coming from you right now. It's amazing. And look." He stuck out his hand and gently rubbed the skin on his fingers.

Vince did not see anything at first, but with a closer look, he noticed tiny hairs sticking out from the pores in his skin. A layer of small tendrils was wrapped around his hands and up his arms. They were even on his face. From afar they looked like hairs, but up close they were new and strange. "What are they?"

"I think it's how I can sense the energy. It's like these things are attracted to it. They want to absorb it."

"This is crazy."

Saul stared down at his hand. "I can't believe it works. I have to try it out."

"What do you mean?"

"I want to drain something."

"Like what?"

"He said it works on trees, right? Let's go find a tree."

Vince looked off into the woods. "Alright, but let's find somewhere a little more private."

They returned to the woods from the night before. The man was gone, but small patches of dry blood were splattered across the dirt. The needle and tube he dropped lay on the ground, leaning against the roots Vince had tripped over. Saul scooped both of them up and studied them closely.

The needle was long but slim. There were two buttons at the top, near his thumb. He pushed the first one, retracting the needle. He pushed it again, and the needle shot back out. The second button sent a puff of air from the tip of the needle. He removed the empty tube and replaced it with the full one.

"What are you doing?" Vince asked. "Why are you loading that thing?"

"I thought you might want to try," Saul answered. He gently flicked the tube and watched the liquid swirl around. With the needle raised, he approached Vince. "Hold still."

Vince pulled away. "Wait. This doesn't feel right."

"Feel right? You don't know how it feels. *I'm* the one who got injected, and I feel just fine. Better."

"We don't even know if it works. If it doesn't, there is no point in injecting myself with that stuff."

Saul examined his face and nodded. "Okay, I'll test it first. If it works, if this thing is real, will you try it?"

Vince hesitated. "Maybe. Do you even know what you are supposed to do?"

Saul retracted the needle and slipped it into his pocket. He walked over to a tree touched it with his fingertips. The hairs on his skin latched onto the bark. "I think so," he said, pulling away and looking at the other trees. "Which one should I try?" There was a small sapling, barely sprouting five feet from the ground. "How about this one? I feel a lot of energy from this one."

"Hmm, how do the other trees feel?"

Saul found another tree, tall and thick, and placed his hand on it. "It has less, but I still feel it."

"Try that one first. We should start small…we don't know what we're dealing with."

"Okay. Here I go." Saul closed his eyes and focused. Vince watched from a distance. He had never seen Saul concentrate so hard. Sweat rolled from his forehead. His cheeks shook as he built pressure in his lungs. Anticipation grew. They both waited, eager to see what would happen next. And then…nothing. Saul opened his eyes and turned to Vince. "Did it work?"

"Do you feel any different?"

Saul shook his head.

"Are you sure you know what you're doing?"

He shrugged. "Maybe the tree is too old."

"I don't think that's the problem," Vince said. "Maybe it just doesn't work. Maybe the man in the suit was lying."

"I really don't think so. These hairs on my skin are real. This feeling I have is real." He eyed the tree again. "Hold on, let me give it another try."

Again, he placed his hand on the tree, closed his eyes, and took deep breaths. And again, Vince watched from a distance. This time, something was different. Saul was calm. Relaxed.

Vince moved his eyes from Saul to the tree. He watched a leaf flutter in the light breeze before shedding off and gently floating to the ground. Its vibrant green descended into a dry, pale brown. A second leaf fell, and a third, and then dozens more. The branches fell bare as a blanket of withered leaves floated down and covered the surrounding dirt. The tips of the branches curled, and the bark peeled in small clumps. Decay crept inward towards the tree's core. Little pieces of rotted bark crumbled from the trunk. Within minutes, the tree was dead.

Saul lifted his hand and turned to Vince, whose face was struck with awe. All of his doubts were gone. Saul smiled. "It works."

"I can see that. How do you feel?"

"I feel good. Really good. I've never felt this good, ever. It's amazing. You have to try it."

Vince, still cautious, was also curious. His attention moved from Saul to the tube of liquid sticking out of his pocket. The man in the suit was telling the truth. Was that even possible? It had to be. He had witnessed it with his own eyes. "Okay. I'll do it."

"Trust me," Saul said, reaching for his pocket. "You'll like it."

Vince rolled up his sleeve. "Does it hurt? It sounded painful when he injected you."

"That was because I wasn't expecting it. It hurts a little, but not too bad. Just a pinch." He held the needle up to his arm. "Ready?"

Vince nodded.

Saul pushed through the skin and pressed the button. The liquid shot out of the tube, into his arm. He flinched but remained calm. He could feel the fluid entering his veins, traveling to his heart, and dispersing across his body.

"Now what?" He asked.

"Now we wait. It takes a while to kick in, but you'll know when it does."

They passed the time with their usual horseplay. Climbed trees, ran around, threw rocks in the nearby pond. And as usual, Vince excelled in each event. He climbed higher, ran faster, threw farther.

Vince picked up a rock. He squared up his feet, tightened his grip, and cocked his arm back, ready to throw. Then he paused, and a smile crept over his face.

"Vince, what's wrong?"

"It's working. I can feel the energy."

Saul clapped his hands together. "I told you. It feels good, huh? And look at your skin."

Vince lifted his hand and stared at the tiny hairs growing from his flesh. "This is crazy. The man was telling the truth. Why would he just give it to us? He didn't ask for anything in return. We're talking about immortality here. That's not something you just hand out for free."

"I don't have a clue, and I don't care. Stop thinking about it and drain something already."

Vince walked up to another large tree and pressed his palm against the bark. He felt the tendril-like hairs latch onto the surface. He closed his eyes and steadied his breath, and in an instant, all of his doubts were gone. He felt the energy coursing through his veins. He was overwhelmed with warmth. With a tingling sensation that filled his heart with glee. The tingling transformed into a powerful force that he grasped with his soul and released through his body.

When he opened his eyes, the tree had crumbled. He was surrounded by a circle of shriveled leaves. Chills ran through his body, from his fingertips to his toes. The feeling was euphoric; unlike anything he had ever felt. The boys exchanged smiles, both speechless.

Saul walked over to the young sapling and wrapped his hand around the top.

"Wait, Saul," Vince said urgently. "Don't drain something with so much energy. Not yet, at least. We're new at this. Take it slow."

"Stop worrying so much. I'll be fine."

As the tree withered and died, Vince saw the pleasure build in Saul's face. The thin trunk of the infant tree snapped off, and Saul stumbled back, overwhelmed. "This sapling, it's much stronger than the other one. Give it a try." he pointed to another young tree. "That one over there?"

Vince shook his head. "No, I've had enough for today. I'll try it later. It's getting dark anyway. We need to get home."

"Go without me. I'll stay a bit longer."

"Okay. Be careful. Don't overdo it."

Vince returned home, feeling better than he ever had. And Saul was left alone, in a forest of energy.

FIFTEEN

ROGER CAME HOME after his first day of school. On his walk back, he dreaded seeing his parents. They were sure to bombard him with questions about his day. Is your teacher nice? Did you learn anything interesting? Did you make new friends? He did not want to deal with these questions. He just wanted to go to his room and read.

But, just as he expected, when he walked through the front door, his mother was waiting. "Hello, sweetie," she said with a cheery voice. "How was your first day of school?"

"Good."

"That's good. Did you make any new friends?"

He lied. "Yes."

She fluttered her hands together in short claps. "That is great news, sweetie! I would love to meet them sometime. I'm sure your father would too."

"I absolutely would!" his father shouted from the opposite end of the room. He was hunched over an open box, rummaging through its contents. "You should invite them over."

"Okay," Roger said.

"How was your teacher?" his mother continued. "Was she nice?"

"Yes."

"Did you learn anything interesting?"

"No."

"Nothing at all? I know it was only your first day, but you must have learned something."

Roger sighed. "I don't know, Mom. Can I just go to my room?"

"Okay, sweetie. You're off the hook for now." Roger darted past her. "But I want to hear more at supper."

Roger shut his door and fell onto his bed. He finally had some alone time. He stared at the bare ceiling for a good while and then sat up to look at the stacked boxes in the far corner of his empty room. He had not unpacked yet, but he was not in the mood.

Instead, he got up and dug through the box on top, throwing piles of clothes over his head until he found the stack of books he was looking for. He placed them on his desk and looked at the top cover. It was a picture of a smiling cartoon turtle.

He ran his fingers over the smooth surface. The title read *The Happy Turtle*. It was a simple, yet appropriate title for one of his favorite picture books as a child. He cracked open the beat-up cover and turned to the first page. Each page had a large picture with text underneath.

He smiled when he saw the rhymes. He enjoyed rhymes. There was a certain satisfaction in finding the perfect pair of words. It was like fitting together the pieces of a puzzle. The first rhyme that popped into his head…*slice and dice*…

He looked down at the page and read the story:

A turtle happy as could be,
Walked down the trail, full of glee.
"The day's a beauty," he proclaimed,
"Just call me Walter. That's my name."

The picture showed the same happy turtle from the cover walking along a dirt path. There were trees on either side of him, their branches full of bright green leaves. The sun shone in the clear sky. He wore a hat showing his name, Walter. It was a simple drawing, but charming. He turned the page:

So on his journey homeward bound,
He smiled big, he smiled proud.
With sunlight beaming on his face,
He kept a slow and steady pace.

There was a cozy house in the distance, presumably Walter's home. He walked towards the house. The sun shone upon his wide smile, showing that he was indeed *The Happy Turtle*.

He looked down at his watch to see,
The time read almost half past three.
A panic overcame his smile,
His first time late in quite some while.

A close-up of Walter's watch displayed the time, 3:30.

Determined to be home on time,
He tried to focus all his mind.
And step by step he made his way,
"I need to make it home today."

The flustered turtle's smile was gone, and in its place, a stiff look of determination. He swung his arms and kicked his knees as he marched down the path, like a soldier in formation.

Despite his efforts and his will,
He moved as slow as standing still.
And soon came fall with colored leaves,
"I hate these slowly moving feet."

Walter had not moved at all from the previous page. The trees still stood by his side, their leaves now an assortment of reds and yellows. Some had fallen to the ground, forming a crunchy trail of autumn colors. He kept his march, but now his face held anger.

From anger came diminished hope,
And now upset, he could not cope.
In desperate cries, he hollered loud,
"Why can't I just be home right now?"

Walter's arms drooped, and his head hung low. All the trees were now bare. The leaves on the ground had lost their color and were an ugly shade of brown. His expression had turned to one of desperation.

> And after fall came winter's hold,
> With heaps of snow and biting cold.
> His body ached, his feet were numb,
> His hope was blown to kingdom come.

Walter stood, more hopeless than ever. His feet dragged with each step. The leaves were replaced with snow, and the sun was hidden behind a wall of clouds, leaving the sky dark and dreary.

This is dark for a children's book, Roger thought to himself as he examined the not-so-happy turtle. But he remembered there was a happy ending.

> And after signs of deep despair,
> A thought popped up, he did not care.
> He realized though he was late,
> It's better to accept this fate.

Walter looked up with a sudden realization. The snow around him was half melted in puddles. Small buds grew from the tips of branches. The clouds had dispersed, and the sun peeked out from behind.

With no more worries on his mind,
He stood and watched the sunlight shine.
Admired flowers here and there,
Enjoyed the freshness of the air.

The page repeated the first image of the book. The green leaves of the trees, the sun shining brightly in the sky, and Walter's big smile.

And after many passing years,
He walked his walk with no more fears.
And to this day, he's full of glee,
A happy turtle as could be.

The final page showed pictures of Walter walking through all of the seasons. A smile plastered on his face, even through the gloomy weather of autumn and winter.

Roger slapped the book closed just as his mother called from downstairs. "Roger, supper is ready!" He stuffed the book in his school bag. He liked to carry it around. It was somehow comforting. As he walked down the hallway, he tried another rhyme...*slice and dice...and something nice*...He could do better.

He entered the dining room and made his way to the dinner table. His father and mother sat on opposite ends, and he took his seat in the middle. On his mother's side, there was a large succulent turkey. The juices dripped from the crispy skin. The steam climbed up into his nostrils and made him drool.

His mother stood up and grabbed the large carving knife and fork. She slowly moved the sharp blade up and down the prongs, making the crisp sound of metal rubbing on metal. Roger watched as she prepared to cut the perfectly cooked meat. *Slice and dice.* She brought the knife downward, slicing through with ease.

Slice and dice, that's one big knife.

She placed a generous portion on each plate. When she was finished serving, Roger indulged his newly-found hunger, stuffing scoops of meat down his gullet. His father watched. "Slow down there, son. You're going to choke to death if you keep up that pace."

Slice and dice, don't end your life.

Roger slowed his bites and sipped his water.

"So sweetie," His mother said. "Tell us more about your first day of school."

Roger sighed. "Must I, Mother? I really am not in the mood."

"Yes, you must." Her tone had a subtle punch to it. "I want to hear about your day."

Roger knew this tone and knew resistance would only lead to trouble. So he told her about his day, but he did not enjoy it one bit.

Slice and dice, she's not so nice.

SIXTEEN

VINCE ARRIVED AT school the next day, refreshed from a full night of sleep. He felt better than he had in years. He entered the room and looked at the clock. Only minutes before class and Saul was still absent. He sat at his desk and tapped his fingers. Ms. Martin walked in and began to teach, but Vince was completely distracted. *There is no way he stayed in the woods all night.* He kept eyes on the door, but Saul never came. As class ended, Vince rushed out of the room and headed directly to the woods.

When he reached the spot from the night before, he saw several dead trees, but no sign of Saul. He wandered deeper, calling Saul's name. There was no answer. He strolled into a small clearing. The sunlight gleamed through past the branches, brightening a patch of green in the grass. At the center of the clearing, Saul slouched over on his knees, head tilted down. In his hands was a dead rabbit, whose frizzled fur had faded.

Vince stepped forward onto dried leaves. The crisp crunch snapped Saul out of his trance. He looked up, and a smile slowly formed.

"Just the person I wanted to see. Vince, come over here."

"Have you been here all night?"

Saul chuckled, "No I went home last night, but when I woke up, I came back."

"I was waiting for you all day. You were just here this whole time?"

"Yes. Although my parents don't know that."

Vince's face held a look of concern.

"Don't worry Vince. I wasn't draining trees all day. I spent most of the time trying to catch this rabbit." He held the carcass up.

Vince turned away. "That's gross Saul. Why are you holding that?"

"I drained it." He said, trying to hold back his smile, but finally giving in. "Vince, it feels amazing. You have no idea. It's better than the trees, tenfold, at least."

Vince recalled the feeling that rushed through his body when he drained the tree. The warmth. The adrenaline. The overwhelming sense of power. The idea of an even greater sensation was intriguing, but he still held reservations. "Are you sure this is okay? It doesn't feel right."

"Why not?"

"You're killing living creatures."

"Don't you realize? This is the key to living forever. We've been handed the gift of immortality. We can't just throw that away. It's like the man said; hunting. We already kill animals to survive. Your father runs a meat shop for Christ's sake. He does this kind of thing every day. Draining this rabbit is the same thing. And look," he held the dangling body up to Vince's face, "now we can eat it. We can take it back to you father to sell. Nothing goes to waste."

Vince listened carefully. Maybe Saul was right. Perhaps he was overreacting. They should use this ability instead of wasting it. It was a gift after all, not a curse. "Okay, show me."

"Yes!" Saul yelled, jumping up with excitement. "Let's get to it then. First, we need to find an animal for you to drain. There are tons of rabbits around. They're just tough to catch. Here, I'll help you."

"I've hunted rabbit before. I know what I'm doing."

"That's what I thought, but there's a catch. Draining doesn't work if the rabbit's dead. You need to catch a live one."

Saul's hunting skills were impressive. He had been practicing all day. When he captured the rabbit, he held it up by the throat. It frantically twisted and turned, trying to escape the tight grasp. Saul wrapped his other hand around the rabbit's hind legs and twisted his wrist. There was a loud snap as the nimble bones in its legs broke. He released his grip and let it fall to the ground. The rabbit wriggled in pain, dragging its legs and rolling from side to side until finally, it went limp. Its chest still puffed in and out and its ear occasionally twitched. Passed out, but still alive.

Saul pointed. "Go on. What are you waiting for?"

Vince picked up the body. He cradled the ball of fur and gently brushed its head with his fingertips.

"Come on Vince! It's not your pet. Go on and drain it already."

Vince did as commanded. He drained the wounded rabbit, and in an instant, understood what Saul meant. It was not necessarily stronger, just different. It was better. From that moment on he was hooked. All of his doubts, fears, hesitations. Gone.

SEVENTEEN

VINCE WAS INTERRUPTED when Horace entered the room. Rupert stood to escort the old man out, but Horace remained calm. There was no yelling or nonsense babbling. He stumbled in and sat in the corner, quiet as a mouse.

"Horace, are you okay?" Rupert asked. "You should be in bed?"

"I want to listen," he whispered.

"Okay," Rupert said, shrugging as he took his seat.

"So, what I saw," Carl said. "That was you draining the horse."

Vince nodded. "That is correct. And I am very sorry you had to see that. It was not my intention."

"What *was* your intention?" Ella asked. "Why did you drain the horse in the first place? That was our only one."

"It was certainly not the ideal outcome. You must understand, I thought Saul was coming. If he was, you would all be dead. I needed to warn you. Protect you. But I was useless in that wheelchair. Draining helps me heal, and I made a difficult decision. I'm afraid it was the wrong one. I hope you can forgive me."

Rupert stared into Vince's eyes. Could he be trusted? "That is quite some story."

Carl nodded. "I liked the story with the turtle."

Turtle.

"The giant tortoise can live for over two hundred years," Ella blurted out. She was not sure why she quoted *The Wonderful World of Animals: Volume 5 — Reptiles*; and now, with everyone staring, her cheeks grew red hot. "I found that quote from a book in the library. I'm not sure why it came to mind."

Rupert patted her shoulder. "No worries, dear."

"I do have one question," she said. "Why is Saul so dangerous? You seemed like really good friends. What changed?"

Vince stared deep into the crackling fireplace. "Everything changed."

EIGHTEEN

Five years went by in Rodin…

NOT MUCH HAD changed in the town of Rodin. Mr. and Mrs. Vigo lived in their quiet house. It was a peaceful town with friendly neighbors. Mr. Vigo went hunting in the woods every day. He butchered the meat and prepared them for sale in his own meat shop, *Vigo's Meats*. Mrs. Vigo spent most of her days looking after the shop, selling the meat to local customers. Occasionally, they traveled to other parts of the Pugg, but most of their business was done in the heart of Rodin.

The day was ending as they closed the shop. He washed his hands and cleaned up while she counted the day's profit. She placed the money into the lockbox under the front counter. Business had been slow for the past few days, giving her time to plan her son's upcoming birthday. In three days, he would turn seventeen. She was planning a surprise party. There were a number of things she needed to do before the big day. Invitations to neighbors and classmates had already been sent. Now, she needed to focus on the final stages of planning. "Honey," she called, "I'm going over to talk with Mrs. Shepherd," she lowered her voice to a half whisper, "about the *you-know-what*."

"Darling, the boy isn't here. You don't need to whisper in riddles."

"I'm just being careful. You never know who's listening. I want to make sure everything is perfect."

"I'm sure it will be," he replied. "You are really outdoing yourself with all of this planning."

"Well, our Vincent deserves it. He's a good boy."

Vince entered through the front door carrying a large bag full of raw meat. "Hi, Father. I have more deer meat."

"Excellent, son. You've been a lot of help around here."

"I like hunting. It's fun."

"Good. Soon you will be doing all of the hunting. I'm getting too old to go out every day."

His mother walked to the front door and waved to both of them. "Bye. I should be back before dinner."

"Where are you going?" Vince asked.

"Just for a walk."

She walked down the stone trail to the road. As she strolled along the side, she came across two lawmen. She recognized one of them: Law Chief Darren, head of Rodin law enforcement. His tall, chiseled figure conveyed strong authority. Next to him was a shorter, much younger man, whom she did not recognize. They both wore lawmen uniforms: simple brown vests over a plain black shirt. Stitched in the corner of their vest was the town crest. A large tortoise climbing a pyramid. The words *Live Free Forever* were printed underneath. Their trousers were loose and baggy. Fine leather straps were wrapped around their waists, equipped with a holster for their batons. They wore wide-brimmed hats, tilted down to block the sun. A silver star was mounted on Law Chief Darren's hat.

As she passed, Darren tipped his hat, "Good evening Mrs. Vigo."

She nodded in return, "And to you Law Chief. On your daily patrol?"

"Yes, ma'am. I'm showing Manny here the patrol route. It's his first day." Manny tipped his hat as well. She responded with another nod. "What brings you outside at this hour?" Darren asked. "You should be home sharing a meal with your family right about now." He gazed up at the sky. "Though I suppose this is fine weather for an evening stroll."

"Yes. It is quite nice out tonight. Although, that's not why I'm out. I'm off to visit Mrs. Shepherd, to make the final plans for my son's birthday."

"Oh yes, of course! How old is little Vincent turning?"

"Seventeen." she answered.

"I guess he's not so little anymore."

"I know; they grow so fast."

"They sure do."

"Are you coming to the party. You're more than welcome."

"I'd love to, but I'll be on duty. Someone has to look over Manny, after all."

Manny tipped his hat again.

She nodded back. "Well, if you change your mind, we'll save a spot for you. Both of you."

"Much thanks, ma'am. Have a pleasant evening."

Manny tipped his hat one last time and followed the Law Chief down the road.

She continued down her path, following the road to its end. Around the corner, two houses down, she saw the Shepherd residence. It was a cozy, one-story building. Its white coat looked freshly painted. A tall brick chimney poked out from the roof. Plain square windows complimented the extravagant red door. She walked up the stone trail and planted three polite knocks. The door swung open to a young boy.

"Hello, Saul. Is your mother home?" The boy wandered off, calling for his mother.

Mrs. Shepherd arrived and greeted her guest with a high cheery smile. "What a surprise. It's so good to see you. Please, come in."

Mrs. Vigo stepped in and slipped her shoes off before following her host into the kitchen. They both took a seat on the wooden stools, facing each other across the table.

Mrs. Shepherd interlocked her fingers and placed them in front of her. She crossed her legs and tapped her foot against the leg of the table. "How are things at the shop?"

"A little slow, but good enough to get by."

"I'll stop by sometime. Your meats are top notch. Best in Rodin."

"Tell that to everyone else. Luckily, we have loyal customers like you to keep our business running."

"I wouldn't even think of shopping anywhere else." She switched her legs to cross the other way. "I don't know how your husband keeps up with it, at his age. The hunts must be exhausting.

"Vincent has been helping a lot. He brings most of our meat now."

"How is Vincent doing anyway?"

"That's actually why I'm here." She leaned forward. "As you already know, his birthday is coming up."

"Oh yes. When is that? In three days, right? I'm looking forward to the party. Have you finished planning everything?"

"Almost. It's a surprise, so I need someone to keep Vincent away from the house while we set up. Saul's a good friend. I was hoping he could take Vincent out for a little while, just to keep him busy."

"He would be glad to."

"Great. Thank you so much." Mrs. Vigo shivered in her seat. "I'm so excited for the party."

"It will be a good time, I'm sure."

"I hope so. Vincent deserves to have a little fun. He always works so hard." They both smiled in agreement. "Anyway, I should get going. Dinner is waiting for me back at the house.

"Very well," Mrs. Shepherd said. They both rose from their seats. "I'll make sure Saul keeps Vincent distracted." She walked Mrs. Vigo to the door and held it open. "Have a pleasant evening."

Mrs. Vigo left with one less thing to plan. The pieces were falling into place. Everything was going to be perfect.

NINETEEN

ROGER WAS DREADING school as usual. Ever since the move to Rodin, he had built up a good deal of enemies. Nobody treated him poorly, they just avoided him altogether. He struggled with school work too. For Roger, school was a place of lonely confusion.

He entered the classroom and walked to his seat in the back corner. When Vince and Saul entered, the only seats open were the two in front of him. They squeezed by to sit down. "Oh great," he heard Saul say. "We have to sit in front of this loser."

"Shut up," Roger said. "I'm the one that has your big head blocking my view."

"It's no wonder you don't have friends. Your parents probably can't stand you."

This was true, and Roger knew it. The last five years in Rodin were the worst of his life. No friends. Irritating parents. He wanted to move back to Vassor but knew that would never happen. *Slice and dice.* Of all his classmates, he hated Saul the most. So when the insulting words left Saul's mouth, his temper skyrocketed. "At least I *have* both of my parents."

As soon as he said it, he wanted to take it back. Saul had lost his father only a year ago and bringing it up now was the most tasteless thing he could have said. Saul's posture sank, and his eyes dropped to the ground. He turned his back and sat down with no response. The surrounding kids glared at Roger. Guilt and anger mixed together to create a whirlwind of confusion in his head. *Saul provoked me. It's not my fault. But everyone's judging me.* Overwhelmed, he reached for his bag and pulled out *The Happy Turtle*. He looked at the image of Walter marching down the trail with a smile on his face. It was calming. He stared at the cover until his mind settled. Once he was calm, he lifted his head to see that Ms. Martin had already started class.

He tried to focus on her words, but could not grasp the material. He needed to refresh his mind. His arm shot straight up, to get her attention. "Ms. Martin, may I be excused?"

"Of course Roger. But don't take too long. You'll miss some important stuff."

Roger placed the book back in his bag and left the room. He paced about outside, making laps around the building. The air was cool and refreshing, and the temperature was just right. The singing birds were soothing. The fresh air was exactly what he needed to clear his thoughts.

As he strolled back into class, Ms. Martin was lecturing on the types of clouds. He returned to his seat and reached into his bag. His book was gone. *The Happy Turtle* had vanished.

His heart pounded like crazy, pumping hot blood to his face. A grinding headache invaded his mind. His hands trembled. His thoughts were incoherent. He twisted around. Looking for the book. Searching on the ground. Under a seat. On a desk. Anywhere. Rage filled his stomach, traveled up his chest, and burned his throat until he could no longer hold it.

"Where is my book?" he yelled, slamming his desk in a sudden rage.

Ms. Martin stopped mid-sentence and stared at Roger, along with the rest of the class. "Where is my book?" he repeated. "I put it in my bag, and now it's gone. One of you took it. Stole it. I know you all hate me. And now you think it's okay to take my stuff!"

"Calm down Roger," Ms. Martin said. "I'm sure no one stole your book. You must have misplaced it."

"No!" He slammed his fist. Tears streamed from his eyes. "I put it down right here. And now it's gone. One of you took it!" He turned and pointed his finger. "It must have been Saul!"

"Don't accuse Saul," she said. "He didn't do anything wrong."

"I'm telling you! He stole my book! He stole it to get back at me for what I said! You know what? Now I'm glad I said it! I'm glad your father is dead!"

"Roger!" She stomped her foot and pointed her finger. Her voice echoed across the room and pierced the children's ears. "That's enough! I will not allow this kind of behavior! You are excused from class! I will have a serious talk with your parents after school!"

"But—"

"But nothing! Leave this classroom, now!"

Roger grabbed his bag and dragged his feet out the door. His face was drenched with tears. How would he explain *this* to his parents?

TWENTY

WITH FIVE YEARS of hunting experience, and plenty of time to experiment, the boys learned much about their powers. They drained mostly deer. It was popular at the shop, and they were common throughout the woods. They had developed unexpected benefits from draining. They could go for long periods without food or water. They needed less sleep and always woke up refreshed. Their cuts and wounds healed quickly, and they never got sick. Their physical strength was at peak form. They took full advantage of these benefits, but they kept their powers hidden, frightened of how others would react.

They also noticed a drop in efficiency. The drains were less potent. The energy from each drain had a lesser effect, as their bodies adapted. To counter this, the boys started to drain more frequently.

It was the night of Vince's birthday party, and on Mrs. Vigo request, Saul took Vince to go hunting, to distract him from her plans. They were both familiar with these woods now. Every path. Every clearing. Every landmark. It was all committed to memory. They knew exactly where to find deer, how to track them, and the best ways to wound them without killing them.

They stood over the body of a freshly drained deer. As they cut the meat with their knives, Vince looked over at Saul and saw intense thought in his expression. "What are you thinking about?"

"What?" he replied, a little startled by the question.

"Something important is on your mind," he said as he began loading chunks of meat into an empty bag. "I can tell. It's been on your mind for a while."

"Oh, it's nothing."

"Nothing, huh?" He adjusted the bag, pulling it towards him. A branch grabbed the side and tore open a large hole. "Damn it. I ripped the bag." He examined the hole and then continued loading in meat. "I know something's on your mind."

"You're not going to like it. Are you sure you want to know?"

"Positive."

"Okay…" Saul took a deep breath. "I want to drain a human."

Silence…

"You can't be serious," Vince said, shocked that his friend could consider such a thing.

"I am completely serious. Think about it. Draining is getting weaker, right? But humans live longer than rabbits and deer. I'm sure you've sensed the energy coming from the people around us. I have too. It feels so much stronger. Imagine the feeling of draining something that strong. I miss that rush that we used to get."

"But these are people you're talking about. It's not for food. It's not for survival. You want to kill for pleasure. You don't see anything wrong with that?"

"You know what I see? Sooner or later these animals won't be enough. If we truly want to live forever, we need to upgrade." He looked at the deer carcass. "If you ask me, there are plenty of human scum out there. People that deserve to die more than this deer."

"If animals aren't enough, what makes you think humans will be. If you start draining people, eventually the same thing will happen." He shook his head. "No. There is no way we can drain a human. If we really want to live longer, we need to drain less. No more draining for pleasure. Only use our powers when we need to. Take a break."

"Take a break?" Saul said. "You want us to stop draining? I didn't expect you to take my side, but this…this is ridiculous. I don't want to take a break."

"You don't want to live for as long as possible?"

"I want to enjoy this gift we have." His voice had grown louder.

"What about living forever?" Vince asked. "Isn't that why we're doing this? I know that's why I am. I don't enjoy killing these animals. And now you're talking about killing people? There's no way we could get away with that. They would catch us. We can't let this get out of hand."

"Maybe it's time for people to know what we can do." He was yelling now. "We can't hide forever. We don't know how they'll respond. Maybe they'll support us."

Saul had a good point. They could never hide it forever. At some point, their friends and family would know. It was inevitable. Perhaps it *was* time to show other people. They would have to plan it carefully. If they did not handle it properly, things could go very bad. Draining a human being was not the proper way to show off their powers. "Saul," Vince said, staring directly into his eyes.

"You have to promise me you will never drain a person…ever."

Saul's jaw tensed up and his breaths shortened. Hot blood rushed from his racing pulse into his trembling face. His frustration built until could not contain it. "Stop telling me what to do!" he screamed, throwing his bag to the ground and stormed off.

Vince was speechless. He sat alone, looking down at the bloody carcass.

TWENTY-ONE

A FTER LOSING HIS book, getting yelled at in class, and being completely humiliated in front of everyone, Roger was dreading going home. But where else could he go? He had no friends. Nowhere to go to stall. And he wanted to tell his parents first anyway, before Ms. Martin could get in touch with them. Of course, nothing could excuse his hurtful words to Saul, but it was not completely his fault. Saul had provoked him. His mind raced as the thought of confronting his parents set in. What would he tell them?

When he got home, he was completely exhausted. He entered the front door and checked the house. "I'm home!" There was no answer. He struggled up the stairs and collapsed on his bed.

*****

When he woke up, the sky was already dark. He had slept through the entire afternoon. He rubbed his eyes and stretched as he yawned. The sound of clattering dishes came from downstairs. His parents were home. Ms. Martin had surely spoken to them by now.

He snuck down the stairs, as quiet as possible. When he reached the bottom, he tiptoed around the corner and into the dining room. His father sat patiently at the dinner table as his mother prepared the food. There was no sign of anger. No disappointment. Maybe she had not yet spoken to Ms. Martin. She held a large carving knife and fork, which she used to slice the juicy ham.

Slice and dice.

She looked up and saw Roger, peeking around the corner. "You're finally awake," she said. She sounded more cheerful than usual. "I was worried you would sleep through dinner. Come, sit down before the food gets cold." Roger approached the table with caution. Did they know about the incident? It was hard to tell. He watched his mother as she cut the succulent ham.

When she finished, she took her seat and placed the knife on the table, near Roger. "So sweetie, how was your day at school?"

Roger stared at his food to avoid eye contact. "Just like any other day."

"Nothing unusual happened?"

"No," Roger said, shaking his head.

"Ms. Martin came by this afternoon. She seems to think differently."

They knew. He needed to explain his side of the story. "Saul started it."

"You told him you were glad his father is dead?"

"I told you. He started it. He said—"

"I don't care what he said or did to you. What you said is completely unacceptable."

Slice.

"You don't understand. Saul has been picking on me ever since we moved here."

"I don't care. You never say that to someone who has lost a loved one. There is no excuse. As punishment, I'm afraid I will have to take your books. All of them. No more reading those ridiculous stories of yours."

Slice and dice.

"What?" Roger yelled. His books were everything. They calmed him down. Helped him relax. Reading made his miserable, lonely life at least a little bearable. He would never let her take them. "You can't do that!"

"Oh yes, I can. From now on, you will come straight home from school. You will study quietly in your room until dinner's ready. No reading. No horseplay."

Slice and dice, she's not so nice.

"Maybe that's a bit much, honey," his father said.

"It is a perfectly reasonable punishment. We raised him better than this."

Roger jumped to his feet. "This isn't fair. You haven't even heard the whole story."

She rose to her feet as well. "You insulted a boy in a completely inappropriate manner." She started to walk towards him. "You were in the wrong. If you can't understand that, then clearly you need to think about it some more. Go to your room."

Slice and dice, I hate my life.

"I'm not going anywhere!" he screamed as she approached. "I'm staying right here!"

She grabbed his wrist. "I am your mother. You will listen to me!" *Slice.* She tugged his arm, but he tugged back. His defiance infuriated her. *Dice.* His father rose from his seat as well, to break up the scuffle, but he found himself caught in it instead. Roger's face burned bright red as he struggled to break free. *Slice and dice.* He screamed with anger. Tears poured from his eyes. *Slice and dice.* He thrashed his limbs back and forth. *Slice and dice.*

And then he saw the knife.

Slice and dice,
She's not so nice,
So grab that knife,
And end her life…

Roger's fingers were tightly clenched around the handle of the carving knife. Fresh blood trickled from the blade's tip. He dropped the knife and pressed his hands to his face, but realized he was rubbing blood into his skin. He lowered his hands and saw two bodies. His mother at his feet. His father hunched over the table. They were both dead.

He panicked. How did this happen? Anger had gotten the better of him. It had taken control of his body. But the anger was not towards his parents. Not even his mother. It was Saul. Saul was the reason his parents were dead.

He grabbed the blood crusted knife and marched out the front door. Tonight was Vince's birthday party. That was where Saul would be.

TWENTY-TWO

SAUL WALKED BACK from the woods, over the hill toward Vince's house. After his argument with Vince, the party was bound to be awkward. He was still upset, but Vince was his friend. He would place his frustrations aside for now, and celebrate his friend's birthday.

He had not planned on telling Vince about his desires to drain a human, at least not yet. He never expected Vince to understand, but he took a chance. Even though Vince objected, he still planned on going through with it. He would still drain a human, just not tonight.

He arrived at the house. The windows were dark, and the only sound was the soft chirp of crickets. Was the house empty? Either that or everyone was really good at hiding. He opened the front door and walked through.

"Surprise!" Lanterns burst with light, filling the room with bright colors. A chorus of people began to sing but stopped when they saw Vince was not there.

"Where's Vincent?" Mrs. Vigo asked.

"He insisted I go ahead without him. He's just finishing up out there and didn't want to keep me waiting. He should be here soon."

"Good." She turned around to face the guests. "False alarm. That was good practice, though. Everyone back to their positions." The people dimmed the lanterns and shuffled back behind the furniture. "How long will he be?"

"I don't know. He shouldn't be too long. Maybe five, ten minutes."

As the time passed, people began to disperse from their hiding to take advantage of the refreshments. Mrs. Vigo had completely outdone herself. The food was delicious, the drinks were refreshing, the decorations were outstanding, and the cake was beautiful. It was a double layer cake topped with buttercream frosting and chocolate sprinkles. She had drawn intricate flowers around the edge, and in the middle wrote, *Happy 17th Birthday Vincent!*

The guests conversed in the dark while Mrs. Vigo peeked out the window. "Are you sure he's coming, Saul?" She held a worried look on her face.

"He said he was. I don't know what's taking him so long."

"Could you go back and check on him?"

Saul did not want to go back, especially after their argument, but he was getting worried, and Mrs. Vigo was starting to panic. "Alright, I'll be —"

"Oh," She interrupted. "I see someone. It must be him. Everyone hide."

The guests returned to their spots behind the furniture. The room went silent as they waited in the dark for the guest of honor. They could hear the footsteps approach the front door. The knob slowly turned. The door creaked open. The shadowy figure stood in the doorway. All of the guests jumped out together, filling the room with light. "Surprise —"

Their festive welcome was cut short and replaced with frightened gasps. The figure was not Vince. It was Roger. He stood, knife in hand. A thick red was splotched across his chest. Sweat and tears ran down his face, mixing with the crusted blood on his cheeks.

Ms. Martin, who was among the party guests, stepped forward and carefully approached him. "Roger, what happened? Are you okay?"

Roger's face was blank. "I killed my parents." His voice was slow and steady. "I murdered them."

She stepped closer, her hands raised in front. "Let's stay calm, Roger. Okay? Could you please put down the knife? We don't want to hurt anyone."

"Saul," he said. "Where is Saul?"

"You don't need Saul right now." She took another step. She could almost reach him. "I need you to put down that knife. Can you do that for me?"

"My parents are dead because of Saul. Where is he?"

Ms. Martin lunged at the knife, but Roger pulled away. As she stumbled, he swiped at her. The blade sliced through her arm and blood gushed from the wound. The others caught her before she could fall.

"Hey!" Saul called out, pushing himself through the crowd. "I'm right here. Leave her alone. She had nothing to do with your parents."

"She had plenty to do with my parents. But I'm not here for her." In an instant Roger was behind Saul, one arm wrapped tightly around his chest, the other holding the knife to his neck. "I'm here for you."

Saul grasped Roger's elbow, trying to loosen his hold, but it only tightened. "Roger, you don't want to do this," He tried to keep his voice calm. "I know you're confused, but think about what you're doing." Warm drops of blood dripped from the blade, its tip poking the skin of his throat.

"I am bringing justice. You're the reason my parents are dead. You're the reason my life is ruined. You must pay for everything you've done to me."

"You really believe that? You think this is all my fault?"

"You stole my book. You provoked me and got me in trouble." His grip got tighter as he spoke.

"I didn't take your book, and I certainly didn't provoke you. You got yourself in trouble."

"Don't lie! I know you despise me."

"I don't despise you."

"Stop lying! Stop lying! Stop lying!"

There was no sense in talking to him. He had made up his mind about Saul. There was nothing he could say to calm him down. "You know what, Roger?" he whispered as he closed his eyes and moved his hand to Roger's bare wrist. "You're right. I do despise you. Always have." His fingers rubbed against Roger's oily skin. "Since the very first time I met you, I hated your guts." The tendrils crept from his fingertips. "You are truly an awful person. Human scum."

The front door opened, and Vince walked through.

"Scum die!" Saul shouted. Energy shot through his arms and into his heart.

"No!" Vince yelled, watching from the door.

Roger dropped the knife and writhed in pain. He shot out a piercing shriek as his limbs contorted beyond his control. Saul held the wriggling body tightly in his arms. Roger's flesh shriveled into a dry crust. His face grew wrinkles, and his eyes rolled back. His hair lost color, turning a thin gray. His screams stretched out to his final breath, mouth wide open across an unfamiliar face. Movement had stopped. The body was just a lump of dead meat.

Saul lifted his hands, letting the body fall to the ground. When he opened his eyes, he saw the guests staring at him. No one spoke. No one moved. No one did a thing. They all just stared. And they all had the same expression on their face. Fear.

TWENTY-THREE

VINCE STOOD IN the doorway, shocked at what had happened. He looked deep into Saul's face and saw unquestionable pleasure. When Saul opened his eyes, that pleasure was replaced with regret. He saw the ones he loved. Family. Friends. They cowered in fear.

He stepped forward, and the crowd backed away. "Wait," he pleaded. "Don't be afraid." He took another step, and the crowd backed away further. "I'm not going to hurt you. Listen to me. Please." He walked towards his mother, her face covered in tears. "Mother." She shook her head and stepped back. Tears of his own began to run down. "You don't have to be afraid. It's just me." She back into a wall and trembled as her son walked towards her.

He reached out and held her arm, but she pulled away and stormed out sobbing. Saul watched her go. "Don't run!" he yelled.

But his yells startled the crowd. They screamed and ran away in a panic. Some went for the front door, some for the back. Others climbed through windows. They did whatever they could to get out of the house, away from Saul.

Through the chaos, Vince and Saul met eyes, standing on opposite sides of the room. They stared at each other as the guests ran back and forth between them. Vince shook his head, and Saul averted his eyes, ashamed.

The room was nearly empty when six lawmen burst through the front door. Law Chief Darren led the squad. They charged in, a baton in one hand and a small shield in the other. They formed a tight circle around Saul and waited for the law chief's orders.

"Men," Darren called, "hold your positions!" He turned to Saul. "Saul Shepherd, you are considered a danger to the public. We must take you into custody. Please lie face down with your hands behind your back. I will only ask once. If you refuse, we will have to use force." Saul did not respond. He stood stiff as a board. Darren raised his hand and pointed forward. They slowly closed in, keeping their batons and shields raised. Once he was close enough, Darren grabbed Saul's arms, twisted them behind his back, and tied them together. Saul did not resist.

They dragged him out, leaving Vince alone in his house. Birthday decorations were scattered about, but there was no one left to celebrate. No friends. No family. They were all too scared of Saul. And that was the moment Vince decided he would never reveal his powers to anyone. The risks were too high.

TWENTY-FOUR

THE DAY OF Saul's trial was a gloomy one. Clouds clustered overhead and the night drizzle grew to a steady downpour by dawn. Fields were muddied, and roads were drenched, but despite the bad weather, a large crowd had shown up to watch. The room was packed. They stood shoulder to shoulder, with no room to move. Vince had arrived early to claim a spot in the front row.

Saul entered the room, and the crowd went wild. His hands were bound as he pushed his way through the mob of people, escorted by Law Chief Darren and two other lawmen. When he reached Judge Porplin at the front of the room, he bowed his head and took a seat at the podium to the right. The lawmen stood against the wall behind him.

The room was thunderous with insults and obscenities. Judge Porplin sat down. His hands rested atop his plump belly, rising and falling with each breath. He watched the clock on the wall as the volume of the crowd grew.

When the hand struck ten, he cleared his throat. "Let us begin!" The room went silent, the people turning their attention to the judge. "Let us begin," he repeated. "Mr. Saul Shepherd. Precisely six days, ten hours, and twelve minutes ago, in the Vigo residence, seventeen-year-old Roger Ramsey was killed. Today, we are here to determine the degree to which you are guilty. Do you understand?"

Saul nodded.

"Please respond verbally, Mr. Shepherd."

"Yes. I understand."

"Very good." He flipped through the papers on his desk, reading the details of the trial, and then looked back to Saul. "Would you like to begin with a statement?"

Saul rose to his feet. "I would like to make it clear that what I did that night was in self-defense. Many of you witnessed what happened. You know this is true. Roger had killed his own parents, and he was going to kill me. If I did not take action, I would be dead. It was life or death. I chose life. Any of you would have done the same." He bowed his head to the judge and took his seat.

"Is that all you wish to say, Mr. Shepherd?"

Saul nodded.

"Please respond verbally, Mr. Shepherd."

"Yes. That is all I wish to say."

"Very good." He flipped through the papers again, reading more carefully this time. "Mr. Shepherd. There is an extensive amount of evidence supporting what you say. Your teacher and many of your classmates confirm that Roger Ramsey exhibited signs of aggression towards you. We found the bodies of Mr. and Mrs. Ramsey in their home, the same night of Roger's death. And we have multiple witnesses that confirm the boy had a knife to your throat. There is no doubt that you acted in self-defense.

Saul sighed with relief.

"However, I would like to make it clear that the focus of this trial is not one of self-defense. We are not here to determine whether Roger Ramsey's death was justified. We are here to sort out exactly how you killed the boy. Some say you strangled him. That there was nothing unusual at all. But most of our witnesses say you possess strange powers. That he dropped dead at the touch of your hand. Some say you're a demon. That you used these powers to torture the boy. Today I intend to find out how much of this is true. We are here to determine if you are a danger to the public. Do you understand?"

"This is ridiculous!" Saul yelled, popping up from his seat. "I am not a danger—"

"Please answer the question so we may proceed with the trial, Mr. Shepherd. Do you understand?"

He sat back down, staring at his hands. "Yes. I understand."

"Very good. Please keep your voice down and refrain from standing, unless you are asked otherwise. Now let us proceed with the trial. I will begin with the schedule. We have already heard a statement from the accused party. Next, we have the speakers. They will help persuade the trial. I have a list of the five speakers here today. Rodney Willis, a witness of the incident. Samara Martin, teacher of the accused party and a witness of the incident. Law Chief Lawrence Darren, the lawman who made the arrest. Doctor William Dillot, examiner of the victim's body. And lastly, Deborah Shepherd, mother of the accused party. Once all have spoken, the accused party will make one final statement, and then I will make my final judgment. Are there any questions?" There was silence. "Okay. Then bring up the first speaker, Mr. Rodney Willis."

The old man next to Vince stood up and shuffled over to the front. He stood in silence, looking up to Judge Porplin for permission to speak.

"Mr. Willis, please tell us what you witnessed on the night of the incident."

The old man nodded. "It was a terrible sight. A terrifying thing to see."

"What did you see?" the judge asked. "Please be specific."

"He had a knife to the boy's neck."

"You mean Mr. Ramsey had a knife to Mr. Shepherd's neck?"

"Correct."

"Please use their names for the purpose of this trial."

"Mr. Shepherd grabbed Mr. Ramsey's hand. That's all he did. Next thing I know, Mr. Ramsey is lying on the ground, dead as a board."

"Is there anything else you recall from the incident?"

"Yes." The man's voice was much softer now. "The look on the boy's face as he died. I'll never forget that look. It was something I have seen only once before and hope to never see again. It was a look of pure agony."

A low grumble spread through the crowd. "Okay everybody," Judge Porplin said. "Quiet down. I would like to keep this trial moving. Mr. Willis, do you have anything else to say?"

The man turned around and raised his arm at Saul. "That boy, the boy you call Saul Shepherd, he's a monster. He cannot live among us. He is too dangerous."

"Thank you, Mr. Willis. You may take your seat. Our next speaker is Ms. Samara Martin."

Ms. Martin filled the spot at the front of the room. She greeted the judge, smiled at Saul, and turned to the crowd. "I was there that night as well. It was truly a terrible night. There is no doubt that Roger's death is tragic." She gestured to Saul. "But are we really prepared to prosecute this young boy for defending himself? Saul is one of my students. I know him very well. I've taught him for over five years now. He is a good boy. A decent person. What he did may have been a little scary, but consider what would have happened if he hadn't. Things would have turned out much worse. Roger was unstable. He had killed his own parents. There was no telling what he would do next. Saul is the reason we're still breathing. He is a hero, not a monster. We should be thanking him, but instead, we are sitting here, condemning an act of heroism."

"Is that all Ms. Martin?"

"Yes, that is all."

"Thank you. Please take your seat. Our next speaker is Law Chief Lawrence Darren."

Darren replaced Ms. Martin at the front. "Thank you, Judge Porplin."

"Please tell the people what you witnessed on the night of the arrest."

"Very well, though I don't have much to report. Our squad arrived at approximately midnight. Mr. Shepherd was standing over Mr. Ramsey's body. My squad placed

Mr. Shepherd under arrest. He did not show any signs of resistance. Upon our investigation, we found nothing unusual about the scene. Doctor William Dillot will go into the specifics of the body." His eyes searched the crowd. "Doctor Dillot," he said, gesturing for him to come forward.

Doctor Dillot stood and took the Law Chief's spot. "Thank you for the introduction. Let me begin by saying, I am quite old. My hair is thinning, and my knees ache far too often. I have practiced medicine my entire life, which, for me, is a long time. I think it goes without saying, that I am very experienced. I have seen some unusual things throughout my career. But this." He held up a folder with Roger's file." This is like nothing I've ever seen before. It is something I cannot explain. So I won't. I will only report what I found."

He opened the folder and glanced over the file before continuing. "I have done some extensive analysis on Mr. Ramsey's body and what I found baffles me. This young boy has accelerated in age. This is not the body of a seventeen-year-old. When he died, he was an eighty-year-old man. Older than myself. I have examined the body multiple times. My colleagues have as well. We all agree, while this may seem impossible, Mr. Ramsey died of natural causes. Of old age."

"Natural causes?" Judge Porplin asked. "A seventeen-year-old boy dies of old age, and you call that natural?"

"Perhaps natural was the wrong word. Please understand, this case is very unusual. But I stand by these results. Natural or unnatural, this is what happened."

"Thank you, Doctor Dillot. You may take your seat." The doctor bowed and returned to his seat. "Now for our final speaker. Mrs. Deborah Shepherd."

Saul's mother made her way up, arms huddled around her body, and stood in front of the judge. "What do I say?"

"Whatever you wish to say, Mrs. Shepherd. This is your time to speak. Tell us about your boy."

She nodded. "In that case, I would like to say that my son is just like any other boy. He plays in the woods, does his chores, goes to school. He excels in school. Isn't that right, Samara?"

Ms. Martin nodded. "One of the brightest students in my class."

"He is a good boy," she continued. "Never causes any trouble. Anyone who truly knows Saul knows that he would never hurt a living soul."

"You were present that night," Judge Porplin said in his stern voice. "Am I correct?"

She began to shiver. "Yes. That is correct. I was there."

"Would you please tell us how you feel about what happened?"

She inhaled deep and let it out slowly. Her shivering grew more intense. Her voice was turbulent. "Obviously, I don't feel good about it."

"Would you please elaborate?"

"That boy, Roger. His life was taken. I know he was holding a knife to my son's throat, but he was still only a child." Her eyes began to water. "No child should suffer a death like that."

"What kind of outcome would you have preferred?"

"I suppose if Law Chief Darren arrived earlier, they could have arrested Roger before any of it happened. That would have been ideal."

"So you are saying what happened with Roger was not ideal."

"Of course it wasn't ideal. A seventeen-year-old boy died. When is that ever ideal?"

"If that is the case, how do you feel about how your son handled the situation?"

She leaned her head back to stop the tears, but they came anyway. "He is a good boy."

"Are you sure? Everyone else is frightened of him."

"They're wrong." Her voice wavered. "He is a good boy."

"Then why would he kill another child?"

"It was self-defense! You said it yourself! That's not what this trial is about! So why are you asking me these questions?"

Judge Porplin bowed his head. "I apologize, Mrs. Shepherd. You are completely right. Let me approach this from a different angle. Your son's actions were justified, without a doubt. How did you feel when Mr. Ramsey passed?"

"I already told you. No one should face such a death."

"You misunderstand my question. I know how you feel *now*, but how *did* you feel, at that very moment. How did you react?"

"I don't know. I froze…and then I panicked, just like everyone else."

"Why do you suppose you and everyone else panicked?"

"Because we had just seen the impossible. There was no explanation for what had happened."

"So you would say that people were frightened."

"Yes," she said. "I suppose you could say that."

"They were frightened of your son."

Her tears began to pool again. "Yes, they were frightened of my son."

"Were *you* frightened of your son?"

She did not answer the question. Instead, she stared at her hands and remained silent. Snot ran from her nose and over her lips, but she did not wipe it away. Silence lingered as they waited for an answer.

"Mrs. Shepherd. Please answer the question."

"…yes…"

"I'm sorry. Please repeat that louder."

Her head burst up in a fiery red as she turned towards the judge and screamed at his face. "Yes! I was frightened of my son!" Tears, snot, and spit sprayed from her mouth as she sobbed uncontrollably. "I am still frightened of my son! Are you happy? Is that what you want?"

They all watched as she lost control. Her screams devolved into meaningless gibberish. The judge signaled to Law Chief Darren, who came forward to escort her out. Her arms flailed and accidentally struck the Law Chief in the face. She rambled nonsense as he dragged her out of the room.

Judge Porplin watched them leave. Once they were gone, he continued with the trial. "All of our speakers have spoken. The accused party will now have a chance to make one final statement. Go ahead Mr. Shepherd."

Saul was haunted by his mother's reaction. To see her break down like that. To hear she was *frightened* of him. After that horrible scene, he could not speak. He had no words. He kept his eyes down and shook his head.

"Very well. Before I make my final decision, I will need some time to myself." He stood from his seat and entered a room in the back.

A rumble of conversation began to build. They were eager to hear his decision. Was Saul really dangerous? Many knew him as the boy Ms. Martin described. A good, hardworking boy. A bright student with a promising future. They had carried friendly conversations with him. He made very good company.

But on the night of the party, they saw a different side of him. His powers were mysterious and frightening. To suck the life from a person with the touch of the hand. To induce agonizing pain as the victim drops like a pile of dead meat. These were chilling thoughts.

Conversation stopped when Judge Porplin emerged and took a seat. "I have given this matter some considerable thought. Mr. Saul Shepherd is obviously a bright boy with good character. It is clear that he killed Mr. Ramsey in self-defense. However, this deadly power he possesses. It is unnatural. Unsafe. For this reason, I am afraid I must deem Mr. Saul Shepherd a danger to the public. He poses a constant threat to every person in Rodin. A threat to all who live in the Pugg. He cannot stay here. Therefore, Mr. Saul Shepherd, I sentence you to banishment."

TWENTY-FIVE

THE VASSOR KIDNAPPINGS began nine days after the trial. Men and women were plucked away from their loved ones in the middle of the night. The wealthy people of Vassor mysteriously disappeared, one by one. No clues. No evidence. It was like they vanished into thin air. News of the kidnappings quickly spread across all regions of the Pugg, and although there was only one reported murder, the others were presumed dead as well.

When the news reached Rodin, Vince made nothing of it. Vassor rarely saw any crime, but these things were common in the lower parts of Rodin. As far as he was concerned, it was none of his business. But when he heard the troubling details of the one reported murder, he was horrified. According to reports, the man had died of old age. But he was not old. He was twenty-eight and had just married his wife. Officials immediately linked the murder to Saul, and within a day, a widespread manhunt was underway.

Vince knew without a doubt that Saul was responsible for the kidnappings, and was likely draining his victims. He had to stop him, or at least try. He snuck out of the house, stole his father's horse, and headed to Vassor.

*****

Everything was a mess when he arrived. Crowds gathered outside, shouting with anger and fear. Troops of lawmen patrolled the streets. Trash littered the ground, tumbling in the breeze. It was not the glamorous town he remembered. The marketplace, which was once a spot for traders and craftsmen, was now populated with lawmen, who marched up and down the perimeter.

Vince tethered his horse and reached down to grab the poster at his feet. It was one of many that were scattered throughout the streets. The top half displayed a rough sketch of Saul's face:

"WANTED:
SAUL SHEPHERD
EXTREMELY DANGEROUS
PROCEED WITH CAUTION
REWARD OFFERED
DEAD OR ALIVE"

He flipped it over:

"CURFEW IN EFFECT:
NO PERSONS SHALL POPULATE THE STREETS
AFTER SUNDOWN
ALL VIOLATORS WILL BE FINED"

They were plastered on every wall.

He wandered the streets and came across a large crowd surrounding a house. They stood behind barriers as lawmen held them back. He approached a young lady near the back of the crowd. "What's going on? Why is this house blocked off?"

She answered without turning. "You haven't heard? There was another kidnapping last night. A man was taken. Five kidnappings in five nights. You know, there are some messed up people out there." She finally turned to peered at Vince. "Should you be out here alone, kid? How old are you? Where are your parents?"

"No, it's okay. I'm seventeen."

"Seventeen, really? You don't look it."

"I get that a lot," he said. And he would get that a lot in the future, as well. People would begin to question his age once he reached thirty and still looked like a teenager. "Five kidnappings in five nights, huh?"

"Yes. It started after that murder. Now someone goes missing every night. They say it's a kid doing all of this. A boy about your age. I hear he has demonic powers. I don't know if I believe that, but you never know. I've heard some weird things about how that man died. Things that only a demon could do."

"Demonic powers?" He tried to act surprised but sounded less convincing than he had hoped. "That's nonsense."

"That's what I thought until I heard what happened in Rodin. The boy killed one of his classmates, just by touching him. No weapons. No nothing. Just the touch of his hand. It sounds crazy, but with all of these stories floating around, it's starting to sound more plausible."

The lawmen waved their hands at the crowd. "Okay people. Clear the area. Nothing to see here." The crowd dispersed.

The lady looked at the lawmen and then back at Vince. "I should get home anyway. Later, kid." She walked off with the rest of the crowd.

She had confirmed what he had feared. Saul was responsible. Now he just needed to find him. He had to be somewhere close, in order to keep returning every night. And nobody had found him yet, so it was somewhere well-hidden. A place no one knew about. A place that was remote and quiet. The cave he told Saul about, the one he used to get away from people. That was the one place that made sense.

He walked along the streets until he found the lawmen horse stables, and snuck around the back. There was the same strange tree he remembered from before, it's trunk split down the middle three ways, almost symmetrically. He examined the twisting roots that burrowed deep into the ground and then continued past the tree where he found the hanging moss. He pushed through the spongy curtain and entered the hidden cave.

He stood by the entrance, waiting for his eyes to adjust. Dripping water echoed off the damp cave walls. The scent of murky water filled his nose and conjured up pleasant memories of his time spent in the cave. He stepped forward, quietly placing his feet on the muddy rocks. He slowly turned his head to sweep the area. The cave was vast, but there was no one in sight. No sign of Saul.

Pathways and chambers branched off from the main route, creating an intricate underground maze. He carefully examined each path when he noticed faint streaks on the ground. Someone was dragged through the mud. He followed the streaks as they twisted around a large pool, and entered a new open area. As he approached a sharp turn in the path ahead, he heard a voice around the corner. He pressed his back against the damp wall and slid closer. His knife hung from his belt, readily available should violence be necessary. He inched towards the corner and stuck his head out. What he saw was frightening.

Five people were bound and gagged. They were slouched over on their knees. They were shaking, from either cold or fear, and they all stared at the ground in front of them. Behind the prisoners was another figure, hidden in shadows, facing away.

Vince stepped out. "Hey!" he called. His voice echoed off the walls and amplified through the cave.

The figure turned around and stepped into the light. A huge smile stretched across his face. "Vince," Saul said. "It's good to see you."

Vince drew his knife and held it out in front of him. "What's going on? Why are you doing this?" He glanced down at the people, who grunted and groaned at the sight of their rescuer. "*What* are you doing?"

"I'm living, Vince. I'm surviving. Simple as that. People don't want me living in the Pugg? Well, the fact is, there's nothing out there for me. If I leave the Pugg, I die.

Banishment is a death sentence, and they know it. They're just too scared to admit that they're sending a kid to his death."

"So you kidnap innocent people? How is that going to help?"

"You said yourself. The people in Vassor are snobs. After spending some time with them, I would tend to agree. They think they're better than us. Why? Because they have a little more money? Because they live in Vassor? Someone needs to show them they're just as pathetic as the rest of us." He glanced down at his victims. As his voice rose, his echo carried beyond the cave entrance, disturbing the horses of the lawmen stables. "These five know. They've had everything taken from them. Their home. Their money. Their family. Now they can see that they're nothing more than scum."

Vince moved forward, his knife still drawn. "Saul, I know you. You're not the monster they say you are, but how is *this* going to convince them that they're wrong? Kidnapping innocent people? Draining them? What you did to Roger was self-defense, but this…this is murder."

"No!" This time, his screams echoed far past the horse stables and reached the main house. A full troop of lawmen prepared to deploy. "I told you! It's survival!"

"Okay," he whispered. "It's not murder. It's survival. So what's your plan now?"

"I'm going to leave. But I need enough energy to survive the flatlands. These five should do. Although I don't know how long I'll be out there. I might need more."

Vince looked at the five terrified faces. "You can't drain them. They're innocent people. It's not right."

"You were right about one thing, Vince. I should have paced myself. I've drained two people so far, and Roger was young. Plants and animals just don't do it for me anymore. If I am going to survive out there, I need humans."

"You can't keep draining people. When will it stop? It's getting out of hand."

Saul grinned. "Vince, things got out of hand a long time ago. Now I'm just along for the ride. This immortal thing is only possible with people. No more rabbits. No more deer. If I have to, I will drain to stay alive."

"I can't let you do that."

"And what are you going to do about it, follow me into the flatlands? You won't survive out there. You've got a good thing going at home. You have a loving family. My time here is over, but you have so many reasons to stay."

"Then I'll keep you from leaving. Then I—"

"Then I'll die," Saul said. "Don't you understand? If I stay, they'll kill me."

"Where will you go?"

"East. I'll follow Harry Hedcrown's footsteps. It's as good a bet as any, right?"

Vince clawed his thoughts for another solution, but every one led to Saul's death. "There has to be another way."

"There isn't."

The soft pitter-patter of feet echoed behind Vince. "Quick!" a distant voice called. "It came from over here!"

Saul's head popped up. "They found me." One of the victims groaned as loud as he could through the gag. Saul jumped down and hit him across the head. "Quiet, you idiot." The other four heard the footsteps and started groaning as well. "Shut up, all of you." He panicked, shuffling back and forth. There was not enough time. He placed his hands on two the heads in front of him.

Vince saw what he was doing. "No! Don't!" But it was too late. Saul drained the two at the same time. They screamed through their gags, writhing in agony.

"Hurry!" the voice said. "The screams. They're coming from over here." The pitter-patter grew louder.

Vince watched, but could not move. He was paralyzed by the savagery. Saul released the bodies and grabbed the next two, but the lawmen were close. There was no time. He kicked them to the mud and looked at Vince. "You've always been a good friend. Goodbye."

A full troop turned the corner, led by Vassor's law chief. "Get on the ground!" Vince dropped to his stomach and placed his hands on his head. They ignored him and approached Saul. "We're taking you in. Don't even think about—" Saul dashed to the back of the cave and vanished into darkness. "Damn it!" He looked at the others. "Don't just stand there! Go after him!" The troop marched past Vince and followed Saul into the shadows.

When they were gone, Vince stood up, wiped the mud from his face, and helped the three remaining victims. When he loosened their gags, he saw nothing but pure terror in their eyes. How could his best friend cause so much sorrow? What happened to the playful, carefree Saul he once knew? The moment they met the man in the suit, the moment they got these powers, Saul changed. The new Saul would continue to drain people. Kill them. His words to Vince were genuine. He would do whatever it took to survive. Vince could not allow that. He could not live his life knowing his friend was out there, spreading fear.

It was night when he got back to Rodin. He snuck into his house to gather some things. Sheets, blankets, dried meat from the shop, a flask of water, and his knife. He stood in the doorway of his parent's bedroom and watched them sleep. "Good-bye," he whispered. "I'll miss you." With that, he left for the flatlands, eastward.

TWENTY-SIX

THE FIREPLACE SIZZLED with dying embers. "So I followed him across the flatlands." The room was captivated by his words. "I have walked for many years. Many lifetimes. Now I go wherever he goes. He has always been one step ahead of me. The night you found me, that was the closest I got, but instead, I found myself thrown off the side of a cliff. Fortunately, Rupert saved my life. But Saul is still out there. I believe he is the one kidnapping your people."

A moment of silence passed.

"So, draining my horse," Rupert hesitated, "that's how you recovered so quickly, right? That's why you can walk right now."

Vince nodded. "Draining has its perks."

Ella shrugged with sarcasm. "You mean other than eternal life."

Vince nodded again. "I know it sounds ridiculous, but yes. I've gotten stronger. Faster. I don't need a lot of sleep. These things developed slowly, but I've been around for a long time."

"And exactly how long is a long time?"

"It's hard to keep track." He stroked his chin as he thought about the question. "I would say a little over two hundred years."

The giant tortoise can live for over two hundred years, Ella thought. She almost said it out loud again but stopped herself. "So, if you've lived for that long," she said, "clearly you're still draining regularly."

"That is correct. I need to stop Saul. In order to do that, I need to survive. And to survive, I need to drain. I try not to drain too often. Unfortunately, plants don't have much effect anymore, but I still stand firmly against draining humans. I drain animals. Rabbits. Deer. Birds."

Fred screeched and flew to the opposite end of the room. She had seen the horse outside and refused to die like that.

Rupert studied Vince's face very closely. Was he telling the truth? Could they trust him? He nodded. "Your story sounds genuine. We will need to discuss this again later, but for now, you have valuable information about our suspect. We need your help, and I think we can trust you. I have one rule, though. You must never use your powers in Snow Peak again. You are our guest, and you will abide by our rules. Understood?"

Vince nodded.

"Good." He beckoned Fred back to his shoulder. She hesitated at first, and then returned, glaring at Vince with a cautious eye. "We can speak with Alan in the morning and decide what to do next. But for now, it's getting late. Let's get some rest.

TWENTY-SEVEN

ELLA STARED STRAIGHT ahead. The sand blew in the wind. She turned her head to see where she was. It was the middle of the desert. A vast land of nothing but sand. Why was she here? She spun around to examine her surroundings. She saw a giant tortoise off in the distance, sitting atop a large sand dune. The great desert creature inched forward, one foot at a time, leaving a trail of massive footprints.

She walked towards it, shielding her eyes from the sun. Up close, the creature was massive. The colossal shell towered over her. She pressed her hand against the rough skin of its leg. It ignored her and continued walking. She grabbed the edge of the shell and climbed to the top, where she sat down to rest. The shell bobbed up and down with each step the tortoise made. She gazed off into the horizon, dangling her feet off the side.

Up above she heard a seagull. She glanced up to watch as it flew by. When she looked back down, her feet were submerged in water, and she was sitting at the edge of a wooden raft. She remembered that she was not in the desert, but in the middle of the ocean. She saw nothing but crashing waves. The raft began to sway as the water roughened. She got to her feet and stood at the center.

From nowhere, she found herself surrounded by a crew of men. They wore brown vests, plain black shirts, and baggy trousers. They all held sharpened knives. In the distance was the distant sound of explosions. The man to her right held a flag that wavered in the ocean breeze. It showed a tortoise climbing a pyramid. "Live free forever," he said with a blank stare. More distant explosions. The waves grew bigger. "Join us. Live free forever, Ella." The raft shook violently, thrown about by the growing wind and water. The explosions grew louder. "Join us. Live free forever, Ella." The waves became too much as she stumbled over. "Join us. Live free forever—"

"Ella…Ella…" Rupert sat at the side of her bed, nudging her from side to side. "Wake up, Ella."

She rubbed her eyes and stretched her arms. "I'm up. What's going on?"

"Alan's ready to talk. He's waiting in the auditorium. Get ready. I'll get Vince and meet you there."

TWENTY-EIGHT

VINCE WOKE UP well-rested. No aches. No pain. It was like he had never tumbled over the cliff in the first place. As he sat up, legs still tucked beneath the covers, there was a knock at the door.

"Vince," Rupert called from outside. "Alan's ready to talk."

"I'll be right out." He quickly changed and grabbed his bag.

Rupert and Fred, who were waiting outside, looked up and down at Vince's new outfit. "You look good. Sure beats those bloody rags I found you in."

"It's a bit large," he said holding out his arm and letting the sleeve hang loose.

"I suppose, but that's expected. Those clothes are mine. I'm a big fellow." He waved his hand and began walking. "Come on. They're waiting for us."

As they walked, Vince looked around. Snow Peak. A nice little village. Cozy. Small. Comfy cabins. Snow covered rooftops. Smoke puffing chimneys…and off in the distance, something caught his eye. Something strange, but familiar. Far off, way up in a tree, was a small metal box, much like the one he saw in Rodin as a child. He had seen these all over the place, and still had no clue what they were. They were always well hidden and just out of reach. This tree, however, looked climbable. It would be difficult, but perhaps he could reach it.

"Hey," he called out, pointing at the box. "What is that? Do you know?"

Rupert stopped to follow his finger. "I don't see anything. Just trees."

"No, look closer. At the very tip. It's a metal box."

Rupert strained his eyes, sweeping the skyline until he saw it, and just barely. A speck in the distance. "Oh yeah, there it is. I have no idea? Never seen it there before." He shrugged. "We can check it out later. Right now they're waiting for us."

When they arrived at the auditorium, the room was almost empty. It felt strange compared to the full house they had for the town meeting. Ella, Carl, Alan's wife Melinda, and Alan himself stood across the room.

Rupert walked forward with open arms. "Alan, my good friend!" he said. "How are you feeling?"

"Much better now that I'm rested."

"I'm glad. We're all so happy you've returned. Now let's get to business." He took a seat in the front row and invited the others to join him. "You have heard the news about Patrick, correct?"

Alan's eyes lowered. "Yes. He was taken the day before I escaped. I saw him."

"What?" Rupert exclaimed. "You saw Patrick?"

"Yes, in the most unfortunate of situations."

"Is he okay?" Ella asked. "Was he hurt?"

"As far as I could tell he was fine, but that can change quickly. That man he's with…he's dangerous."

"That is why we must find him as soon as possible," Rupert said. "Did you see the man's face? Can you tell us anything that will help?"

"I will tell you exactly what happened, from the moment he snatched me from my bed."

TWENTY-NINE

ALAN WAS USUALLY fun and lighthearted, but now he spoke with a serious tone. "That night I awoke in fear, to a dark figure standing over me. His details were hidden in shadows. Melinda was still asleep. He had gagged me and bound my wrists and ankles. I tried to break free, to wake up Melinda, but it was no use." He looked to his wife as they joined hands. "The man held me down and leaned in close to my ear. His voice was deep and raspy, and his words were chilling. 'If she wakes up, she dies. Go ahead. Wake her up.' After hearing those words, I stopped fighting. I tried not to move, but my body still trembled.

"The man picked me up and threw me over his shoulder. He carried me out of my cabin and into the woods. The cold seeped through my clothes and numbed my skin. My head hung behind his back, and all I could see were his feet. He left no footprints. Special shoes I guess. The metal clang of keys jingled from his belt. He walked for a good while, until sunrise, and then finally placed me down in the snow. I turned my head to look around, and what I saw was frightening. We had passed the edge of the woods and entered the snow plains. The sight of white fields stretched for miles. Sitting in front of him, protruding from the flat ground, was a cage."

"A cage?" Rupert interrupted. He turned to Vince with a questioning look. Vince shrugged. He was just as surprised to hear Saul had a cage.

"Yes," Alan said. "A cage. Large with thick metal bars. It was about half the size of a cabin, and it sat on six wheels. At the front was a metal seat with controls on the side. It had only one door, slightly smaller than a normal door, that was secured with a hefty lock. Inside the cage were people, prisoners from other parts of the world."

"How many were there?" Rupert asked.

"When I arrived, twelve. They all looked very weak."

"Why would he keep them like that?" Ella asked.

"So he could drain them," Vince answered. "He's saving them for later."

Alan furrowed his brow. "Drain? No, he was bringing us somewhere. A place called the City. He kept mentioning it. 'They'll take good care of you in the City,' he would say."

Vince tilted his head, confused. "The City? What's the City?"

Alan shrugged. "I don't know, but that's where he was bringing us."

"How did you escape?" Ella asked.

"I got lucky. The night after, I was sitting inside the cage with everyone else. The man was gone. He had come back here. It was dark and cold in that cage. A typical night around here I suppose, but I had no coat. There is something particularly eerie about the empty snow plains at night. Its vastness frightened me." He looked at the faces in the room. They had all seen the snow plains at night, and they all agreed, even Fred. "We waited for him to return. We feared that he would leave us. That we would freeze to death.

"But he didn't. As the moon rose, the man emerged from the woods, with another body upon his shoulder. It was Patrick. He was unconscious. The man dropped him in the snow and reached for the keys on his belt. He unlocked the cage door and bent down to pick Patrick up again. But as you all know, Patrick's not the lightest guy around. The man struggled with his body. This opened a window of opportunity for me. I charged at the unlocked door and busted through. I fell to the ground, hands and feet still bound. Lying there, I had no idea what to do next. I had no escape plan. I was acting purely on impulse. When the man saw me, he jumped on top of me before I could wiggle away. I fought back, trying to shake free, but I was tired, and my body was weak. That's when the cage door slammed open. The prisoners flooded through, but the opening was too small. They all pushed against each other, stuck in the opening as the door swung freely open.

"The man let go of me and ran to the door. While he fumbled with the cage, I got to my feet and hopped over to Patrick, who was lying in the snow. I nudged him, but he was out cold. There was no way I could carry him with my hands bound. I had no choice. I had to leave him. I glanced back at the cage to see the prisoners holding his keys. The man pushed against the door, trying to keep it shut.

"It was the perfect distraction as I hopped toward the woods. I dived behind a tree and glanced back towards the action. The man had his keys back on his belt, and the prisoners were now secured. He walked back to Patrick, turning in my direction. I tried not to move, but the cold snow made it difficult. I clenched my chattering teeth. My breath was short and erratic. The man came closer. I could hear him speaking to someone. Maybe just himself. 'You lost him?' he said. 'How could you lose him?' His words were filled with rage. I froze, praying he wouldn't see me. He stopped at Patrick's body and bent down to pick him up.

"As he carried him back to the cage, turned away from me, I crawled deeper into the woods. The dense branches blocked the sky, and the thick bushes hid the ground. I rolled into a bush. He must have heard the rustle because he placed Patrick down, turned around, and peered into the woods. His eyes darted from side to side, scanning the thick bushes. He wandered closer, his eyes searching through the dark. He walked right up to me, the tread of his shoe in front of my face. I held my breath.

"And that's when Patrick woke up. The man took one last scan of the woods and turned around to put Patrick in the cage. He yelled at the prisoners to stay back and shoved Patrick inside. He locked the door, sat in the front seat, and tinkered with the controls. The cage moved forward atop the six giant wheels. I watched from the bush as they disappeared into the snow plains.

"Once they were gone, I rolled out and tried to sit up. I rubbed my wrists against a tree and managed to free my hands, although the bark scratched them up pretty good." He held up his wrists to show streaks of red across his skin. "I freed my ankles and walked into the dark woods.

I found myself lost in the woods for a good day, but eventually, I made it back."

"What did this man look like?" Rupert asked.

"I didn't get a good look. He wore a hood which kept his face hidden. He was a large man. Tall and built. I know that's not much."

"It is still helpful," Rupert said. "But there's something more important. Do you remember how to get to this cage?"

Alan nodded and pointed east. "That way. I can show you."

"You've been through a lot. Are you sure you're ready to go back out?"

"Yes," he answered, without hesitation. "If it means rescuing Patrick, I'm happy to help."

Rupert patted Alan on the shoulder. "Very well. We will leave this afternoon. And Alan, it truly is good to have you back."

THIRTY

AS THE OTHERS gathered equipment, Vince sat on a bench and peered up at the metal box in the tree. The precise edges. The smooth, shiny surface. The circular glass which was pointed in their direction, as if it were watching them.

Rupert walked by with his arms full and saw Vince staring into the trees. He placed the bags down and took a seat. Fred, who was still scared of Vince, hopped over to his opposite shoulder. Rupert peered up at the box. "That thing really has you curious, doesn't it?"

"It does."

"It is strange, no doubt. Never seen a thing like it."

"I have seen many, but none this close. They are always far out of reach. But this one…"

"You mean to retrieve it?"

"Perhaps." Vince turned to look at Rupert. "Do you think it's possible? To climb that tree?"

Rupert studied the tree from top to bottom. "It is a tall one. The branches are scarce, just like the ones around it. It would be difficult. Perhaps impossible. But you climbed up the side of that cliff, something I also would have called impossible."

"You're right about the branches. It would be a challenge." He looked up again. "Could Fred fly up there? Get it down for us?"

Without responding, Rupert stood from the bench and raised up his arm. Fred jumped from his shoulder to his hand. "Go ahead girl. See what that thing is."

She let out a shriek and launched from Rupert's arm. She dashed towards the tree with her talons ready. The wind frizzled her feathers as she soared through the air. Once she was close, she slowed her speed and hovered over the box. She tilted her head to examine the object and grabbed the metal with her talon. A loud crack echoed through the air. Pain shot up her leg and through her body. Her wings stiffened, and she plummeted down like a rock, spinning through leaves and branches. She gained control fluttered her wings to slow her fall, but it was not enough. She slammed to the ground with a solid thud.

"Fred!" Rupert screamed. He sprinted to the base of the tree and Vince following closely behind. Fred got to her feet when she saw Rupert, and let out a reassuring chirp. "You're okay?" Rupert whispered. He stroked her head. "Don't scare me like that."

When Vince caught up and saw that Fred was okay, he tilted his head upward. "That's weird. I don't feel any energy from this tree. Like it's not alive. Not real."

Rupert brought his face an inch away from the trunk. "It sure looks real to me."

"It is convincing," he said as he touched the bark, "but it's not like the other trees. It's different. Artificial."

"You mean someone built this tree and placed it here?"

"I have no idea. It makes no sense." He turned to Rupert. "I'm going to climb up."

Rupert shook his head. "Back there I thought it might be possible, but from here, it's just too tall. There are no branches up near the top. And once you get up there…if you get up there, it will shock you just like it shocked Fred."

"Not if I don't touch it. You don't understand. I have traveled the world for longer than I can keep track of, and everywhere I go, I see these things, these boxes. They're hidden. They're out of reach. But I see them. And now I have a chance to get up close. I need to know what they are."

"How do you plan to get up there?"

"The same way I got up that cliff." He unsheathed the knife and grabbed another from his bag. "With these." Rupert looked unsure. "Trust me. I was weak on that cliff. But now I'm rested. Well fed. I'm stronger than I was back then." He approached the trunk. "I'll be fine."

He secured his bag, tucked a knife into his belt, and gripped the other with his teeth. He hopped up to grab a low branch and pulled himself up. He carefully placed his feet as he scaled the base of the tree, the branches becoming more scarce the higher he went.

He was up higher when a branch snapped from under his feet, and he quickly grabbed another one overhead. He dangled, looking up at the branch that he gripped. The base was slowly bending, beginning to crack. The lower branches were sturdy, but up here they could not hold his weight.

With his free hand, he grabbed the knife from his mouth. He stretched his arm back and thrust forward, fixing the blade in place. The branch snapped off and slipped out of his hand. He held the handle of the knife as his body swung down and slammed into the bark. He grabbed the other knife from his belt and climbed up the tree, just like he had climbed up the cliff.

The rest of the climb was no trouble. When he reached the top, he waved down to Rupert, who waved back. Fred let out a triumphant call. She must have been rooting for him despite her earlier reservations.

He turned to the box and admired the ornate craftsmanship. There was a faint humming noise. He tilted his ear and inched closer. The humming was coming from inside the box. He pulled his head back and stared for a moment. The glass piece in front was large and circular. He leaned over to look through the glass but saw only darkness. It was tempting to grab it, but he knew it would shock him. If he could grip it long enough to tear it off its post, he could drop it from the tree and examine it more closely once he was back down.

He toyed with the thought when he noticed wires sticking out from the back, feeding into the tree. With the tip of his knife, he tapped the metal surface. Sparks flew, and a loud crack echoed. He flinched but kept his balance.

He looked at the wires again and placed his knife on the rubber lining. With one quick slice, he cut through the wires. The low hum silenced. He tapped the blade to the surface again and...this time nothing happened. No sparks. No loud crack. He stored away his knives and inched his hand forward, carefully running his fingertips along the metal surface. Nothing happened. No pain. No shock.

He grabbed the box with both hands and pulled, but it would not budge. The base was mounted to the tree. He rubbed his palms together, and grabbed the box again, this time pulling with great force. The bark splintered, and the box broke free. He held it out, staring with wide eyes. He looked down at Rupert. "I got it! I'm coming down!" He threw the device in his bag and began his descent.

When he reached the bottom, Rupert peeked into his bag. "How did you manage that?"

"There was a wire." Vince pulled it out to show him. "Right here. It was powering a security system of some sort. It should be safe now." As he said this, Fred hopped up and pecked at the box.

Rupert examined the strange artifact. "What is it? It looks just as foreign down here as it did up there."

"I don't know, but it must be important. Someone didn't want us to find it."

"We should take it apart. Figure out what it is. What it does."

Vince nodded. "Yes, I agree, but not until after we catch Saul. This box can wait, but Saul is getting farther away."

"I agree. Let's finish packing. The day's almost half gone."

Vince stuffed the box in his bag and went inside to help the others pack.

THIRTY-ONE

ELLA AND ALAN sorted through the village supply shed, stuffing their bags with equipment. Melinda stood in the corner folding her husband's spare clothes. "Do you really have to go out again? You just got back. Surely you can spend a few days to rest first."

"No honey," Alan said. He continued sorting without looking up. "Patrick is still out there. This Saul guy still has him locked up in that cage, and every minute we wait they get farther away. We need to leave now." He lifted his eyes and looked into hers. "I hope you understand?"

"Of course, I do. It's just, that morning when I woke up and you were gone, that was the worst day of my life. I don't want that to happen again."

Ella walked over to Melinda and rubbed her back. "Don't worry. Your husband is in good hands. We'll all be there to look out for him."

"I know, Ella, but still… Saul sounds really dangerous. We have no idea what he's capable of. And this Vince fellow. Do you really think we can trust him? Do we know anything about him? He's a stranger, nothing more."

"He is a stranger. That's true, but I do trust him. He knows Saul. He grew up with him. Maybe he can reason with him."

"And what if he's lying to you?" Melinda said, shaking her head. "What if he's leading you into a trap? What then?"

"I honestly believe we can trust him. Rupert agrees, his story sounds genuine. But I suppose only time will tell."

Alan took his wife by the hand. "We must find Patrick." He held her in his arms, and whispered, "Rupert will be there. He'll look after us. We'll be fine."

"Just be careful, okay?" She wrapped her arms around his head and pulled in closer to hug him.

"Ella," Alan said. "Have you told your mother you're leaving? I can't imagine Tamara will take this news well."

She sighed. "Not yet. I'm sure that will be fun. I'll go tell her now." She grabbed her bag and left.

A minute later Rupert, Fred, and Vince entered the room. "Are you ready Alan?" Rupert said in his jovial voice. "It's time to go. Where's Ella?"

Alan, who had just finished packing, lifted his bag over his shoulder. "She went to say bye to her mother. But I'm all set and ready to go."

"Very good. We can wait for Ella outside."

THIRTY-TWO

VINCE WATCHED THE others say goodbye to their loved ones. Alan to his wife, Ella to her mother, and Rupert to all the others. There was a strong sense of community in Snow Peak, something Vince had given up the day he left Rodin. All his family and loved ones had perished long ago, and now he was tracking down his best friend, to kill him.

When goodbyes were done, they turned their backs to Snow Peak and entered the woods. They carried large bags on their shoulders. Rupert led at the front of the group. "So Alan," he said, "which way do we go?"

Alan pointed straight out. "You've got it. Just keep going straight." He looked to Ella. "How did your mother take the news? Was she upset?"

"Of course she was. You know how my mother is."

"You've always been there to look after her. It's hard for her to let you go."

"She was upset, but she understands how important this is."

"Melinda is the same way. She hates that I'm leaving so soon, but she supports my decision. I guess that's all we can ask."

"I suppose so," Ella replied softly.

"What about you, Vince? Have anyone waiting for you back home?"

"Alan, don't..."

Vince raised a hand, "It's okay, Ella. He doesn't know. Home for me is far away. I haven't been there in a long time. My family has passed. Friends too. Really all I have is Saul..." They stopped walking. A somber silence filled the air. Then Vince looked up and smiled. "And of course, I have all of you." They chuckled and started walking again. "It's true there aren't many people in my life, but it's nice in its own way. It's peaceful."

"You must have met other people in your travels," Ella said. "I can't imagine we're the first ones you've come across."

"There were others, but only in passing. I never stayed in one place too long. No more than a day. I'm constantly moving to keep up with Saul. He moves fast."

"And then you found us," Alan said.

"Yes, I found Snow Peak."

"Why did you stick around so long?"

"My feet were torn up. I couldn't walk. If I could, I would have left right away."

"And when you catch him, what are you going to do? Kill him?"

The question rang in his ears. Would he kill him? Could he bring himself to kill his only friend?

Rupert interrupted before he could answer. "We'll worry about that later. Let's focus on getting there first. Alan, would you lead the way?"

"Yes sir," He jogged to the front, with Ella walking by his side.

Rupert fell back to speak with Vince. "The two of you must have been close. You and Saul I mean."

Vince nodded. "Yes. Very close." He raised his eyes to look at Rupert. "He's not going to stop. He will resist, and given the opportunity, I believe he'll kill me." His eyes dropped down again. "But I don't know if I can kill him."

THIRTY-THREE

AFTER HOURS OF walking, they reached the edge of the woods. The terrain opened up to a vast field of snow. The snow plains. Alan looked around. "It was somewhere around here."

Rupert walked up beside him. "Let's sweep the area and see if we can find anything."

They all walked off in different directions to search for clues. Fred flew up high to get a better view. It did not take long for her to spot the trail in the snow. She shrieked and flew towards the tracks. The others looked up and followed her lead.

Rupert crouched beside the lines in the snow, leading out towards the snow plains. "Well, it looks like he made it easy for us." He pointed his finger out. "He went that way. We'll follow, but first, we need some rest. The sun is low and the night will get dangerously cold. We shouldn't be outside for that. When the sun rises, we can follow these tracks."

They had two tents; one for Vince and Ella, the other for Alan, Rupert, and Fred. After pitching the tents, they entered the woods to gather firewood.

Night fell, and they huddled together. A kettle of beans hung over the crackling fire. As they ate, Vince retold his story. Ella and Rupert had already heard it, but it was important for Alan to know about his powers, and his relationship with Saul, as well.

When his story was done, Alan's reaction was one of disbelief. "Two hundred years? You're telling me that you and Saul are two hundred years old." He darted his eyes from one face to another. "You all actually believe this?"

"He's older," Rupert said. "And yes, I do believe it. This draining business may sound farfetched, but Carl saw it with his own eyes. And Vince's feet are healed. That's all the proof I need."

"I assure you," Vince said, "I'm telling the truth."

"Amazing," Alan said. "How can anyone live for so long? It's ridiculous."

Ella turned to Alan. "The giant tortoise can live for over two hundred years."

They all looked at her. "Why do you keep bringing that up?" Rupert asked as he scooped more beans from the kettle.

"I don't know. I read it in a book, and that sentence stuck with me."

Alan ignored Ella and continued with his thought. "You drained his horse, huh? Can you drain something else? That is something I would like to see."

Rupert nodded. "Yes. I would too."

"Me too," Ella said, raising her hand.

Fred shrieked and hopped to Rupert's other shoulder, away from Vince.

"Easy girl," Rupert said. "He isn't going to drain you." He turned to Vince. "You said it works on trees. Drain that one."

Vince looked at the tree. "I suppose I can if it helps convince you that I speak true." He stood up and placed his hand on the trunk. "Are you ready?"

The others nodded.

The tendrils stretched from his skin, burrowing into the bark. "Okay, here it goes." He closed his eyes and started draining. Leaves fell until the branches were bare. Cracks formed near the base of the trunk and worked their way up. The bark crumbled off to reveal the rotting core. The colors faded to shades of ash. Within seconds, the tree had gone from vibrant and beautiful to hollow and dull.

An empty shell of what it once was. When he was done, he opened his eyes and turned to face them.

They had all risen to their feet, speechless. Even Fred's beak hung open. They had never seen something so hauntingly beautiful. They stared at the tree, and then at Vince. He was grinning. "Alan, I'll take your silence as a sign of belief."

"Belief?" Alan yelled. "I feel terrible for ever doubting you. That was incredible!"

Rupert placed a hand on his shoulder. "Calm down, Alan. It was indeed incredible, something I hope to learn more of in the future, but it's getting late. We need sleep. We leave as soon as the sun is up."

"What?" Alan exclaimed. "I can't sleep after seeing something like that."

"Try. We have a long day ahead. You'll need all the rest you can get." He tugged Alan's arm. "You're with me. See you two in the morning."

Vince and Ella put out the campfire and entered their tent. Vince opened his bag and pulled out the metal box.

Ella glanced at the device as she climbed underneath her covers. "You're not going to sleep?"

"I'm not tired. I'm going to spend the night taking this thing apart."

She picked it up and turned it around in her hands. "What is it?"

"I don't know, but I intend to find out. Rupert and I found it in a tree back in Snow Peak." She yawned as he spoke. "I won't keep you up, though. I'll do it outside."

He grabbed the device and opened the front of the tent. "No," she said. "I want to watch. Now I'm curious." She plucked it out of his hands and studied it's shiny surface more closely.

He sat down next to her. "Okay, if you insist."

"If you had to guess, what do you *think* it is?"

"I've seen them all over, but never this close. Perhaps some kind of monitoring device."

"Monitoring device?" She held it to her ear. "Who would want to monitor us?"

"That's the question, isn't it? It must be someone powerful. These things are all over the world. Someone well-traveled." He grabbed it back and tinkered with the cut wire sticking out the back. "Someone that doesn't want us to know they're watching." He pulled out his tools. "Now let's get started."

*****

By morning, they had fully disassembled the box. All of the parts were splayed across the ground. Ella helped sort the pieces. "Organization is key," she had said and insisted on forming different piles for different types of parts. The first contained exterior parts. The six metal plates that formed the outer shell, a cylindrical piece that extruded from a hole in the front, and the wire that Vince had cut. The second pile held an assortment of curved glass parts, mostly pieces from the inside of the front cylinder. The third pile held the larger interior pieces. Plates with strange patterns on them. And the final pile held the smaller interior pieces, consisting mostly of tiny gears.

Vince placed his tools down and leaned back to admire their work. "And that does it."

"What do you think it is now?"

He looked at each pile carefully. "I still don't know. I have never seen anything like this before."

"Me neither."

"It is very advanced, no doubt. And it has a defense system." He held up the wire. "It almost killed Fred before I disabled it."

"So whoever placed it up there didn't want us to find it." She picked up an interior piece and turned it in her hand. It was nothing special. Just a rectangular metal plate. As she placed it back down, she noticed something in the corner, under her thumb. It was a small gold colored symbol. She brought it close to her eye, but it was too small.

Vince handed her a curved piece of glass. "Use this."

She held it up to magnify the symbol. Printed in gold paint were two overlapping ovals, one slightly angled to the right. A large "C" sat in the center, with the words "City Property" engraved below. She smiled and handed it over. "See, being organized helps. Take a look."

He examined the symbol. "City property, huh? Well, it's our property now."

"What is City?" Ella asked.

Vince placed the piece down. "Alan heard Saul talking about it, right? He said he was taking them there."

"Why would this City place plant this device in Snow Peak?"

He shrugged. "Not just in Snow Peak. They're planted all over."

The front of the tent opened up, and Rupert walked in. "I see you two are already up." He looked at the mess on the ground. "And you took apart that box."

Ella jumped up with excitement. "We figured out where it's from."

Rupert placed his hand on her shoulder. "That can wait. The sun is almost up. Pack up. We need to get moving. You can tell me as we walk."

Before she could argue, Rupert was gone. She looked at the four piles. "So much for being organized." They scooped the pieces together and dumped them in an empty pouch. Vince threw it in his bag and helped Ella disassemble the tent.

THIRTY-FOUR

THEY WERE PACKED and up walking as soon as the sun peeked over the snow. The cold wind blew as they followed the tracks deeper into the snow plains. Alan turned to see their progress. The woods in the distance were just a small speck now. He turned again to look at the snow tracks, stretching far ahead into nothingness. "Hey Vince, how long do you think we'll be out here in the middle of nowhere?"

"Hard to say. All we can do is follow these tracks."

"But we could be walking for days. Weeks even. How do we know when to stop?"

Vince glanced at Alan. "We never stop. We keep walking until we find him. A day, a week, a year…whatever." He stopped walking and turned to face the others. "I hope you all understand. I will not stop."

Rupert nodded. "Yes, we understand. We will stay with you for the time being, for Patrick, but you must understand that we have lives back in Snow Peak. We have loved ones waiting for us. And we will return home." He looked to see if the others agreed. Both Ella and Alan nodded. "We'll stay with you for now, but if we don't find him, we'll have to go home."

"I understand. I must say, I am starting to like this little group we've formed. The company is nice. I very much enjoy your presence, and I hope you feel the same."

Alan walked up behind Vince and patted his back. "Of course we do, buddy. I only just met you, but I can tell you're a good guy."

Ella grinned. "Yeah Vince, you're our friend. No matter what happens, you're always welcome to visit us." Fred left Rupert's shoulder and flew over to Vince, rubbing her face against his cheek. Ella chuckled. "It looks like Fred likes you too."

They all laughed.

They started walking again. Vince noticed a set of footprints alongside the tracks they were following. If Saul was riding the cage that Alan described, why would there be footprints? "Were these here before?"

"No," Rupert said. "They were not. I noticed them as well. Do you suppose Saul has a follower?"

"Perhaps. I imagine he has many enemies."

"Maybe someone got lost out here," Ella said, "They might be following the tracks in search of a town."

"I suppose it's possible, but where are they coming from? The only place around here is Snow Peak."

"We should continue on this path," Rupert said, "but with caution. We know Saul is dangerous, but this second person could be even more dangerous."

Someone more dangerous than Saul. The thought frightened Vince.

THIRTY-FIVE

THE NEXT TWO days were quiet. They walked. Ate. Slept. Vince had many stories to pass the time, tales of his early years, about his troubles as a child lost in the vastness of the open plains. He enjoyed telling stories to his new friends. He had traveled in silence for so long, it was nice to have people who were willing to listen. Occasionally, Ella and Alan would share a story from Snow Peak, and Vince was fascinated. Rupert barely spoke at all. He told no stories. He only listened, a wide grin peeking through his beard.

The third day in the snow plains was not as pleasant. It was horrifying.

The day began just like the first two. The five woke at sunrise, packed their bags, and walked along the tracks. They discussed languages and the difference between Snow Peak's dialect and Vince's Pugg speak. The two were remarkably similar. Grammar was almost identical, but there were minor differences in vocabulary.

"Pelon," Vince said, "a word I presume you have never heard, is a unit of measurement. It measures distance. An inventor from the Pugg coined the term. Rodin's very own Harry Hedcrown.

"Hedcrown?" Ella raised her head as the name caught her ear. "That sounds familiar."

"Yes. I mentioned him earlier in my story about Saul. He left the Pugg to explore the outside world, but he never returned. In Rodin, he was an inventor. The pelon came from an experiment of his. He was testing the limits of the human body." Vince stroked his chin. "I believe a pelon is the average distance a person can walk in a day."

"How far is that?" Alan asked.

"I don't recall. It once held truer meaning, but now I use it as more of an expression. On a slow day, I say I walked a bad-pelon. On a good day a good-pelon."

"What about an average day?"

Vince did not respond.

"…Vince?"

Alan waved his hands to get his attention, but Vince just stared off into the distance. They turned to see what held his eyes, but there was nothing but the same white snow. Fred, with her excellent eyesight, was the only one who knew what he was looking at, and the sight was terrifying. She shrieked with panic, fluttering her wings and hopping about Rupert's shoulder.

"Woah, calm down girl," Rupert said. "There is nothing to worry about. Everything's just fine."

Fred knew that everything was not just fine as she stared with Vince at the scene up ahead.

Vince saw blood but said nothing to the others. There were no words. They would have to see it themselves. At a distance, it was hard to tell if the blood was Patrick's. He watched the red splotch grow larger as they got closer, and waited to see who would notice first.

"Oh no," Ella cried as she jogged ahead.

Alan reached out. "Ella, wait!" He followed right behind her.

Rupert and Vince stayed back, maintaining a calm stride. Rupert watched as Ella and Alan ran off. "Is it bad?"

"It's hard to say," Vince said, staring straight ahead. "There is a lot of blood, but it may not be his."

"We can only hope."

When they reached the scene, Ella and Alan stood over the red snow with terror on their faces. Written with blood were the words *STAY AWAY*. Above, was a severed hand, propped upright as if it was waving at them.

"That monster," Alan muttered.

Vince studied the hand. "Do we know this is Patrick?"

Ella pointed to the blue ring around the pinky. "Yes. That's his ring. Martha has one just like it."

"What should we do?" Alan asked. "Do we listen to the message?"

Rupert swiped his hand, dismissing the idea. "Absolutely not. Saul knows we're following him. This is his way to scare us off. I am frightened, no doubt, but this gives us even more reason to continue. Now we know how dangerous this man is. How far he is willing to go. Sure, if we persist we risk putting Patrick in even more danger." He paused to think about his next words. He wanted to get them right. "But if we do as he says, if we stay away, Patrick is gone forever. We have an advantage. We outnumber him. And we have Vince." He patted Vince on the shoulder. "We can rescue Patrick. I know we can. And I'm not going to let some pathetic threat like this scare us off."

"That's right," Ella said. "There's no way we're going to turn around now. This Saul guy doesn't realize who he's dealing with."

They turned to Alan, who chuckled. "What? Do you even need to ask? Of course, if you're in I'm in. Let's get that son of a bitch."

Vince smiled. "Good, we all agree."

They continued walking, past the bloodied hand.

*****

The next morning, it happened again. They marched through the snow when Vince stopped. "Oh no. Another one."

Again, Fred fluttered in a panic. Rupert looked, but there was nothing to see. "Is it Patrick?"

Vince did not respond. Again, Ella and Alan ran ahead, while Vince and Rupert stayed back. Arriving at the scene, they found another hand. This time, written in blood, *LAST WARNING*.

Alan looked to the others. "We're still going, right?"

They nodded without question. *Of course we're still going*, Alan thought. *He couldn't scare us off yesterday. What makes this any different?* But deep inside it felt different. It was stronger. Scarier. The idea that Patrick could die. Or was already dead. This unsettling thought festered down in his gut as he followed the others along a path of uncertainty.

THIRTY-SIX

THE FIFTH DAY was warm. Patches of yellow grass peeked through the melting snow. Their surroundings grew lively as they neared the edge of the snow plain. Birds. Rabbits. Shrubs. Trees. After days of nothing but snow, it was nice to see some change. But once the snow was gone, the tracks were gone as well. There was no more trail to follow.

After an hour of wandering in what they hoped was the right direction, they came across a cave, protruding from the face of a small mountain. They stood at the mouth, peering into the darkness. The walls stretched deep until shadow swallowed them whole.

Vince examined the cave, and memories from the past reappeared. He remembered that day in the cave. The day Saul had drained those innocent people. The day he left the Pugg. It was a long time ago, but the memories were still vivid. He remembered the dull cave walls, the moist smell, the hollow silence. This cave, the one that stood before him now, was just like the one from his past.

Alan gazed at the others. "What are we—"

Vince shushed him and cupped his hand behind his ear. "Listen," he whispered.

They all leaned forward. There was almost nothing, almost complete silence. Almost. But from the deepest corner of the cave they could hear a faint sound. Voices echoing from the cave's inner depths.

"Is that Saul's voice?" Ella asked. "Do you recognize it?"

Vince listened a bit longer. "It's hard to tell. It's very soft, and I haven't heard his voice in a long time. I need to get closer to be sure."

"Okay, then," Alan said. "Let's go." He began to walk forward.

Vince held him back. "I'll go first. It could be dangerous." He held a finger up to his lips. "Try to be quiet. If we're lucky, we can sneak up on him."

He entered the cave. The dark was overwhelming, but his eyes adjusted quickly. The sound of each step echoed off the jagged walls. The air grew warm and wet as they ventured further in. Puddles of murky water were scattered across the ground. They listened carefully as they walked, hoping to hear Saul's voice again. They heard nothing but dripping water.

Up ahead, the cave split into three paths. They all stopped to look at Vince. He cupped his ear again and tilted it forward. This time, there were two voices. One was possibly Saul. The other was familiar, but hard to place. It was a voice he had heard before. He pointed down the middle path and led the group deeper.

The voices grew clearer as they walked. He was now certain of Saul's voice. Torchlight bent around the corner ahead. The looming darkness lifted as they moved closer to the light. They approached slowly, anticipating what was around the corner. Both excitement and terror pounded in Vince's heart.

Would Saul cooperate? Probably not. Vince was sure of this and was prepared to deal with such. It was the second voice that made him uneasy.

He pressed his hand against the cave wall and peeked his head around the corner. Saul held a torch above his head, facing the other direction. Across from him stood a dark figure, and behind the figure, a cage. A tarp was draped over the metal bars, hiding its prisoners. The figure was tall and well built. He wore a large hooded cloak which hid his face in shadow. Only his pale lips were revealed by the dim glow of Saul's torch.

"I can't let you leave!" Saul yelled. "You know that."

"Sure you can," the man responded. "It is a very simple task." His voice was raspy, yet still familiar. "Saul, my friend, this is what I do."

"Don't call me that. I'm not your friend. We barely know each other."

"On the contrary, you may not know much about me, but I know quite a lot about you. You are one of our specimens after all. We keep all of our subjects under close surveillance, especially those beyond the walls. It would be unprofessional otherwise." He paused, as if a voice spoke to him in his head. His thin lips stretched into a wide grin. "I'm sure Vince knows what I mean. Don't you Vince?" With no response, the man chuckled. "I know you're there, Vince. You and your friends can come out." Vince stepped around the corner, out of hiding. The others stood behind him. "It's good to see you again, Vince. I heard you found one of our cameras. I'm impressed. That tree was a tall one. You've grown strong over the years." He turned back to Saul. "I can't say the same about you, Saul. It's interesting how different the two of you have come along."

Saul stared at Vince with wide eyes. "Vince…"

Vince glanced at him and then back to the hooded man. "Who are you? How do you know who I am?"

"Oh Vince, I'm disappointed. Don't you recognize me? I suppose it has been a while. Maybe this will help." He lifted his hood to reveal his face. A patch covered his left eye.

The sight of the eye patch instilled shock. It was the man from his past who changed his life forever. "You're the man in the suit."

"Ha! Is that what you called me back then? I suppose I did wear a lot of suits in those early days. I have to admit, I looked quite silly in those small suits. Fortunately, that name no longer fits me, as you can see," he spread his arms to display his hooded cloak, "and I don't think *man in the hood* is quite as catchy." His posture was sturdy and strong. He was not the clumsy mess Vince remembered. "Please, call me Mr. Carbul. Or better yet, Barnabus. No need for formalities. We all know each other here."

"You don't know us," Ella said.

"Of course I do, Ella." She flinched at the sound of her name. "As I said, we keep *all* of our subjects under close surveillance. And as I'm sure you know by now, Alan here has caused me quite a bit of trouble." He glared intensely into Alan's eyes. "But all is well. I'm not one to hold grudges."

"I don't understand," Vince said. "What's going on?"

Saul shook his head. "I tried to tell you on the mountain, but you never gave me a chance to explain."

"Explain what?"

"It's not me you should be after." His voice lowered. "He's the one doing all of this." He pointed to Barnabus.

"But those people you killed in Vassor. You—"

Barnabus chuckled. "Yes, I remember that day. I must admit, that was quite a surprising turn of events. Very amusing to watch. Unfortunately, he didn't keep it up for long. It's a shame. I was rooting for you, Saul. You embraced your power. You pushed it to its limits. None of this self-righteous mumbo jumbo like you," He turned to Vince. "Saul realized that you were better than the others. He realized that I gave you a gift, and he showed appreciation for that gift, but you had to drag him down, question his morals. Do you know what morals are for? The weak. He stopped draining people and look at him now. A pathetic excuse for a man, withering away, a victim of time."

Vince looked at Saul with hopeful eyes. "You stopped draining people?"

Saul nodded. "That's a decision I made a long time ago. But not soon enough." His head dropped in shame. "I attacked two towns after Vassor. That is something I'm not proud of." He looked up and pointed to Barnabus.

"Then I ran into him. He told me things. Things that you should know."

Barnabus laughed again. "Frankly, I'm surprised you never figured it out on your own. They told us you were Rodin's brightest. Perhaps even brighter than that Hedcrown fellow. I was honored to be your contact agent. But you were just a disappointment. Greene insisted that you had potential, but I knew right away you would let us down."

Vince placed a hand on Saul's shoulder. "Saul, what did he tell you?"

"He said we're test subjects. Lab rats."

"No," Barnabus said, "you're not lab rats. We have other subjects back in our lab. We let you roam free. You're more like…field rats."

Saul ignored him. "We were chosen as subjects, and that man was assigned to give us the formula. That day back in the woods, he *needed* us to take it. That's why he was so persistent. They wanted to observe us. They're still watching us right now."

"Who are *they*?" Vince asked. Saul looked to Barnabus for an answer.

"*They* would be my superiors. Greene and all of his lab guys." He smiled. "You know, they're watching right now. That's how I knew you were following me. I presume you saw my messages."

Alan stepped forward. "We got your message, you bastard. You don't scare us. Now hand over Patrick!"

"Ah yes. Patrick. Your friend from Snow Peak." He began to pace back and forth. "You know, Snow Peak has caused me a lot of trouble. It was such a simple job. Collect the rats and go home. Bring the lab guys their new batch of subjects. I was so close too. Just across the water at the end of this cave. It's important work you know, and I take it very seriously. Great things come out of our research. Technology, transportation, medicine." He lifted his foot. "Even these snowshoes. You may find it hard to believe, but I consider myself a savior of lives. Hell, you two wouldn't even be alive right now if it weren't for me. It's truly amazing, the steps we've taken towards everlasting life. People fear death. They think it's the end, but that's not true anymore. We are entering an age of *no* end, and you two were some of the lucky souls that got to taste it first." His pacing was now faster, more anxious. "You know, I could be home right now, eating a nice hot meal with my family," his raspy voice dropped lower, "but I had to deal with Snow Peak. It started with you, Alan. You had to break out of my cage and get the others riled up. I suppose it's partly my fault. I got sloppy. I left the door unlocked. But after you escaped you sparked somewhat of a rebellion. They tried again and again to escape, led by your very own Patrick."

"Where is he?" Alan insisted.

"I'll get to that, but you must be patient."

Alan walked forward. "I don't have to be anything. You're going to tell us where the hell Patrick is and—"

"Enough!" Barnabus commanded. He reached behind his back, pulled out a device, and pointed it at Alan. A loud thunderous echo shot from the object. A clump of dirt shot up from the ground and into Alan's face. Alan froze in place. Fred fluttered about and shrieked in fear. The sound traveled throughout the empty cave, dying down until there was silence. "It's time you all realize that I am the one in charge here. You will listen to what I say. No interruptions, otherwise, I'll let this gun do the talking."

They all stared at Barnabus. What was this gun device? It appeared to shoot thunder. It was a frightening thought; that thunder could be harnessed and used as a weapon.

Barnabus continued his speech, now with the gun pointed at Alan's head. "As I was saying, Patrick, that hot-headed moron, decided to take charge and rally up the others. He slowed me down considerably. He was the reason this persistent little rat," he gestured to Saul, "was able to catch me. He was a problem that needed to be dealt with. You saw my first attempts to silence him. Unfortunately, I underestimated his ability to endure a few dismemberments, so I took things a step further.

"You didn't..." Ella started but stopped when she remembered the gun.

"Yes, Ella. You've got it right. I killed him. Beheaded to be exact. I don't want to skimp on the details. Don't hold it against me, though. He forced my hand. I had no choice."

"Oh please," Saul said, stepping in front of Alan, into the line of fire. "Don't blame this on your prisoners. You enjoyed it because you're sick." He waved for the others to move back. Ella, Alan, and Rupert obeyed. Vince remained where he was. Saul took another step forward.

Barnabus steadied his arm. "Don't come any closer. I don't want to shoot you."

Saul took another step. "I don't buy that. I think nothing would make you happier than to shoot me right now. But you can't, can you?" Another step. "Your boss, this Greene fellow, he needs us. They're not done studying us." Another step. "Every muscle in your body wants to kill me right now...but you're not allowed to."

Another thunderous bang crashed through the air. A warm red mist splattered into Vince's face. Saul dropped to his knees, clutching his stomach. A red splotch spread from under his hands. A gargle of blood filled his throat as he struggled to breathe. Fred let out another panicked shriek. Smoke danced around the hot barrel of the gun, in front of Barnabus' angered face.

Vince ran to Saul and knelt down beside him, catching him in his arms before he hit the ground.

Barnabus flashed his deranged smile. "You're wrong about two things, Saul. First, you overestimate your importance to our research. You two aren't the only ones with the formula. We have plenty of other subjects that have abilities just like you." He walked over to the tarp that was covering the cage, waving the gun carelessly as he spoke. "Second, no one tells me what to do. Greene doesn't control me. He doesn't even respect me. I know about Project Monika. I saw Trish sneaking around in the labs. If he's not going to keep me in the loop, I don't have to listen to him." He raised his arms up and yelled at the walls. "You hear that? I don't have to listen to you!" He lowered his arms back down and grabbed the tarp in his fist. "If I want to kill Patrick, I will. If I want to cut all of Greene's subjects into tiny little pieces, no one can stop me." His lips formed a grin. "See?"

He pulled the tarp off in one swift motion. The center of the cage held a bloody mess. Severed arms, legs, torsos, heads. Blood dripped from the pile of flesh, pooling around the metal floor of the cage. At the top of the pile, staring straight ahead with dead eyes, was Patrick's head.

"Like I said, I do whatever I want." He saw the terror in everyone's face. It was exactly what he was hoping for. "And If I want to kill all of you…then that's exactly what

I'll do." He pointed the gun at Vince, ready to strike thunder into his chest.

But Fred reacted like lightning…and lightning is faster than thunder.

She sprung from Rupert's shoulder and darted at Barnabus. She dug her talons into his fingers and shrieked into his face. The gun shot once, hitting the dirt next to Vince, before falling to the ground. Barnabus swung his arms, trying to swat Fred away, but she held her grip. Finally, he grabbed a hold of her wing and threw her aside. She slammed against the wall and fell to the ground.

"Fred!" Rupert ran forward. Ella and Alan followed.

Vince left Saul's side and trotted over to pick up the gun. He cradled it in his hands, uncomfortable with the power it granted him. Barnabus approached with pure rage in his face. Vince pointed the gun. "Stop!" Barnabus ignored him. "I said stop!" His shouts were pointless. It was clear that he would not stop. Instead, he walked faster, eyes glaring at Vince. He marched right up to him and reached for the gun, when finally, Vince pulled the trigger.

Barnabus fell like a rock. Blood pooled around his chest, staining the ground with crimson darkness. His arms grasped at Vince's legs. Vince stepped back. Adrenaline pumped through his veins. His breathing grew heavy. He pointed the gun down at Barnabus once more and unleashed a barrage of thunder. Blinding light flashed from the gun with each shot. Spurts of red sprayed from the body. He pulled the trigger until the deafening blasts were replaced by a soft click.

Bloody mangled meat and bones lay on the cave floor. Splatters of red covered Vince's face and chest. The others watched as he glared down at the body. Ella approached him with caution, reaching out slowly, placing a gentle hand on the gun, and carefully pulling it away. His eyes darted up. With the sight of Ella, he snapped out of his trance.

Ella handed the weapon to Rupert, who threw it in his bag like a hot potato. He walked over to Vince and patted his back. "Are you okay there, son?" Vince gave a slight nod.

Saul was still on his knees, coughing and spitting up blood. Vince and Ella ran over to help. Rupert and Alan stayed with Fred, who was quivering in the corner. She stretched out her wing to reveal a large gash. Rupert picked her up and held her close to his chest. The beat of his heart calmed her. "You did good, girl. You saved us."

Saul was not doing well. Blood gushed from his wound, his face was ghost white, and his body was drenched in sweat. Vince retrieved the sheet from his bag, placed it on the ground behind Saul, and cradled him onto his back.

Ella pressed on the wound as Saul cried in agony. She held her hands firmly in place. "Sorry hun," she said in her most comforting voice. "I know it hurts, but it's for your own good." Saul ignored her and continued to scream. His body twitched and squirmed in a violent motion. Ella struggled to keep her hands still, but the man saved their lives. Now it was their turn to save his. His struggling weakened until he finally gave up and accepted the pain. "Rupert, I need a bandage?" Ella called. Rupert pulled out a roll from his bag and tossed it over.

As she wrapped the wound, Vince peered into his old friend's tear filled eyes. "Hang in there, friend. Don't quit on me now. You've always been strong."

Saul stared back. "Vince, I'm scared." His voice was barely a whisper. "I'm terrified. I don't want to die…We were supposed to live forever…" His voice trailed off, and his eyes rolled back. Vince held him close to feel his heart beat. He was still alive.

"He passed out," Ella said as she finished patching the wound. "He lost a lot of blood. It's a miracle he's still alive."

Alan walked over to look at the man who came between him and the gun. The man who saved his life. And the man who was now on the ground, dying in his own pool of blood. "We have to help him!" he said. "We can't just let him die!"

Rupert shook his head. "There isn't much we can do. We don't have the supplies to handle such a wound, and Snow Peak is five days off, at least."

"There must be something we can do!" Alan turned to Vince. "He's your friend! Let him drain you or something! He'll heal faster, right?"

Vince carefully cradled Saul back down. "Unfortunately if Saul drains me, or any of us, he will kill us. It is impossible to drain without doing so."

Alan pointed to what was left of Barnabus' body. "Well then drain that son of a bitch!"

"He's already dead," Vince said with regret. "We can only drain the living." He looked at the body, riddled with countless holes. How could he be so stupid? How could he let emotions erase the only way of saving his friend? He could have shot once. Kept Barnabus alive.

Ella stood up, wiping the blood from her hands. "What about the City," she said. The other looked at her curiously. "He said the City has the best in medicine. And it's not far either, just across the water at the end of the cave. That's what he said, right?"

"I believe so," Rupert said.

"Then let's go! What are we waiting for? We can save him, I know it. We owe it to him. We owe it to Vince!"

"Yeah, let's go!" Alan yelled. "We have to try!"

Rupert was less enthused. "We must not let our emotions get in the way of reason. I'm not saying we can't try to save him, but we must think carefully before we make any decisions." He stroked Fred's beak, who was quivering in his arms. "I don't want anyone else to get hurt."

They looked to Vince, who was staring at his friend on the ground. "I would not ask you to follow me into the City. We don't know what's there. It could be dangerous. There could be others like Barnabus. You may return to Snow Peak if you wish. You have all become close friends. It will be sad to see you go, but I must try to save Saul."

Alan leaped in front of Rupert. "Come on, Rupert. He stepped in front of the gun. That could be me on the ground right now. If that was the case, we would already be halfway through the cave by now. He risked his life to save ours." He placed a hand on Vince's shoulder. "Vince needs our help."

"And Patrick," Ella said. "We'll do it for Patrick."

Alan looked at Ella and launched back with even more passion. "For Patrick! We need to stop whatever those bastards in the City are doing." He pointed to the cage, full of bloody limbs and torsos and heads. "We can't let this savagery go on!" He locked eyes with Rupert. "So what do you say? Are you in?"

Rupert returned a deep stare and then looked down into his arms. "Fred here is hurt pretty badly. It sounds like the City can treat her wound as well. To the City we go."

Alan sprung up and hugged him. Vince and Rupert exchanged smiles as Alan ran over to help.

THIRTY-SEVEN

WITH VINCE'S SHEET and some branches, they fashioned together a makeshift stretcher. Vince held the front near Saul's head and Alan took the back. They followed down the cave path as it led them to sunlight, opening up to a vast beach. Waves washed onto the rough sands of the shore. The calm breeze carried a salty smell that was oddly pleasant. Seagulls circled above, occasionally nosediving into the ocean.

Alan stared at the water. "How are we supposed to get across that?"

Vince shrugged. "When he said across the water, I wasn't expecting this." He looked to Ella and Rupert for suggestions.

"Look," Ella said, pointing down the shore. "There's a boat."

They all turned and saw a large unoccupied boat. Its metal sides were smudged with dirt. On the back, the words *CITY PROPERTY* sat above the same golden symbol they had found on the camera, crusted with dried salt.

"It must be how he got here," Vince said, "and how he planned on getting back."

They walked across the beach, towards the boat. The sand made it tiring to walk. Their shoes filled with small grains and pebbles. When they reached it, Rupert climbed the ladder leading up over the side rail. "Wait out here," he said. "I'll make sure it's safe." The others placed Saul gently on the ground and looked around.

Ella peered across the water. "I've read about the ocean before, but I've never seen it in person. It's beautiful."

Alan picked up a rock and skipped it across the surface. "I don't know. It's looks kind of scary to me. What about you, Vince?"

"I find it peaceful. It can get rough out there, dangerous even, but nothing beats a sunny day on the calm waters. It will be nice to get away from the snow."

Alan snickered. "Getting sick of the cold weather, huh?"

"I haven't seen such temperatures in my travels. I'm not used to it."

"You definitely grow a tolerance when you grow up in Snow Peak," Alan said. He nudged Ella. "Isn't that right Ella?"

She nodded. "You sure do, but you get a little stir crazy, as well. I'm excited to see what's out there. Something other than home."

Rupert emerged from the boat. "It's safe. The boat's empty."

They climbed aboard, extra careful with Saul in their hands. They placed him down, and Vince began to wander off. "Can you watch him? I'm going to look around."

Ella gave a thumbs up. "I'll keep an eye on him."

The boat was bigger than he expected. There were two stories, each with multiple rooms. He could tell the boat was old. The metal floors were dirty and rusted, and several windows were broken. On the first floor, he passed by what looked like a pantry. The cupboards were filled with boxes of food and water, enough to last a month at least.

Near the front of the boat, still on the first level, the floor had a large indent. In the corners were deep slots, perfect for holding large wheels. It was mostly likely how Barnabus transported the cage.

Vince turned right and found a spiral staircase. His boots clanged on the metal as he climbed up. The second floor was just as run down as the first, but with hints of luxury. In a lounge-like area, there were splintered hardwood floors, covered with a beat up red carpet. Large paintings hung from the walls. Portraits of unknown people. Four bright yellow chairs sat at the center of the room, all facing each other. He walked over and sat down. Dust puffed up from the cushion, filling his eyes and lungs. It was not clean, but it was comfortable. After a moment of rest, he stood up and moved to the next room.

The bedroom was small but cozy. There was a single bed tugged in the corner, with a wooden nightstand beside it. A circular window on the back wall lit the room with sunlight. He sat on the bed and more dust filled the air. After a short coughing fit, he got up and moved on.

At the front of the boat was the control room. The wide window showed a stunning view of the ocean. There was a large panel against the wall. Buttons of various shapes and colors were spread across the board, and levers were scattered about. He was overwhelmed by the cluttered mess. Instead of experimenting with them himself, he returned downstairs to tell the others.

As he came back down the spiral staircase, Alan and Rupert were exploring the pantry, and Ella was sitting cross-legged on the floor next to Saul. "What did you find?" she asked. "Anything good?"

There's a good amount of food in there, but it looks like Rupert and Alan already found that. There's also a bed upstairs. It's a good place for Saul to rest." He walked over and bent down to lift the stretcher. "Help me get him up the stairs."

They lifted Saul and brought him up the winding staircase. Alan and Rupert followed behind, fascinated by the second-level decor. They had never seen a place like it. The place was dirty and rundown, but to them it was beautiful. The carpet. The colors. The paintings. It was all beautiful.

They carried Saul through the lounge and into the bedroom. He moaned incoherent blabber as they transferred him over to the bed. His face had lost color and faded to a pale shade of peach. A slick layer of oil coated his skin, and his entire body was shivering. The red splotch on his bandage had grown.

"He's not doing well," Ella said as she patted his forehead with a cloth. "We need to get him to the City fast."

Vince nodded and turned around. "Rupert. Alan. Follow me." He led them to the control room. "We need to figure out how this works."

Alan stared at the controls. "How in the world are we supposed to do that? There are like a hundred buttons here. For all we know, one of them could set the boat on fire!"

"It's possible," Vince said, examining one of the levers. "They have pretty impressive technology."

"What's that supposed to mean? I'm not going to press anything if it has the function to kill us!"

"He's joking," Rupert said.

"Really? You're always so serious, Vince. It's hard to tell. Good one, I guess? You could work on your sense of humor, though."

"I'll keep that in mind," Vince said as his hand hovered over the controls.

"Just push one already," Rupert said. "We don't have all day."

He pushed the orange button in the very top left corner. They all waited and listened, but nothing happened.

Alan chuckled. "Of course it's not the first one we try. I think we all knew that."

Vince pushed the blue one next to it. Nothing. When he pushed the third button, they heard a loud click coming from the front of the boat below them. They looked out the window to the deck, where the cage was supposed to go. He pushed it again and the same sound emitted from the corners. There were small latches the locked in and out of place whenever he pushed it.

"That must secure the cage in place," Rupert said. "To make sure it doesn't roll around or go overboard."

Alan laughed. "That would make for an interesting ride. Just imagine that gigantic cage rolling around. That creepy guy would have had his hands full."

On button number twenty-four, they heard a hum coming from the back of the boat. They listened closely until the boat nudged forward. They were off the beach and headed into the ocean.

"It's about time," Alan sighed. "I thought I was going to lose my mind."

Through trial and error, they learned how to steer. There was a horizontal lever that turned left and right, and a vertical one that controlled the speed. They still had no clue what most of the buttons did, but all they needed was full speed, straight ahead.

Now that they were on a smooth course, Vince looked back towards the bedroom. "Keep an eye on the controls. I'm going to check on Saul and Ella."

Alan took control. "You got it, boss."

When Vince entered, Ella waved for him to come over. "Quick," she whispered. "Get over here. He's waking up."

Saul struggled to open his eyes, squinting as Vince came into sight. "Vince?" His voice was weak. "Is that you?"

Vince reached out to hold his hand. "That's right old friend. I'm here."

Ella stood up. "I'll give you some privacy."

When she was gone, Saul grabbed Vince and pulled him down for a hug. "I missed you."

"Me too, Saul. It's been a long time."

"Where are we? What happened to Barnabus?

"He's dead. I shot him with his own weapon. We're on his boat and headed to the City now."

Saul smiled. "Good riddance. That bastard deserved to die. After all these years it's finally done."

"It's not over yet."

"You're right. The City. They have a whole lab of prisoners. And who knows how many *field rats* are out there?"

Vince flinched at his use of the term. "Don't call us that. We're not rats."

"To them we are. We're nothing more than experiments."

"That's why we have to stop them."

"I know."

"What else do you know about the City? About the people there?"

"Not much. I know they've been watching us from the start. They've got those cameras set up all over the place.

"I noticed them too."

"Barnabus kept talking about Victor Greene. I think he's in charge of their whole operation, maybe even the leader of the City. Either way, he's powerful. Dangerous."

"So he's the one we go after next."

Saul nodded. "Whatever he's up to, it's no good." He clutched his stomach and groaned. "You can't imagine how much this hurts."

Vince placed his hand on top of Saul's. "We'll get you to the City. They'll fix you up there."

"What if they don't? What if Barnabus was right? If there are other subjects like us, they don't need us. There's no reason for them to save me."

"We have to try."

"Vince, I'm scared." His eyes began to water. "I've been scared my entire life. Afraid of death. And now it's coming. I can feel it. I'm going to die."

"No, you're not. We are going to save you."

"And then what? We can't keep this up forever. Somewhere down the road, we're going to die."

"That may be true, but death is a part of life. We live. Do what we can. And then we die. Everyone dies."

"Not us." Tears ran down Saul's cheeks. "It was supposed to be different for us. We were promised immortality. But I can see that's not real now. That draining is wrong. People were not meant to live forever. I keep telling myself that I drain because I have a purpose. To stop thieves. Murderers. The scum of the world. But what if that's not my purpose? What if it's just an excuse? I've been grasping for life in pursuit of a better world, but when we succeed, when we stop this Victor Greene fellow, will we stop draining? I don't know if I have the courage."

Vince smiled. "You've changed so much. I can tell by the way you speak. When the time comes, I have no doubt you'll find the courage you're looking for." He stood up and walked to the door. "Now get some rest. I'll wake you up when we reach the City."

As he left the room, he thought of Saul's words. Draining was wrong. They both knew it. And yet they both continued to do it. Vince had never considered that he was afraid of death, but maybe he was. When the time came, would he have the same courage Saul was looking for? He was not sure.

THIRTY-EIGHT

THEY TOOK TURNS watching Saul. It was Alan's turn. Ella, Rupert, Fred, and Vince stood in the control room, peering out at the ocean. There was nothing but blue waves and blue skies. Two seagulls flew beside the boat as it cruised across the open waters.

Ella gazed at the horizon. "I didn't know the world could get so beautiful."

Rupert nodded. "It's easy on the eyes, that's for sure."

Ella pressed her hand against the glass. "I've only known a world of cold snow. There's so much out there I haven't seen." She turned around. "What do you think the City is like? It sounds so different from Snow Peak."

Vince nodded. "It does. It sounds big. They have impressive technology. It will most likely be very different from Snow Peak."

"What are we going to do when we get there?" She asked.

"We'll have to wait and see. They might welcome us with open arms. Or they might try to kill us. Either way, they know we're coming. Of that much I'm certain."

"What do we do if they fight us off?"

Vince and Rupert answered together. "We fight back."

Rupert walked forward. "We've come this far. There's no point in running away now. Like you said before, Saul risked his life to save ours. Now it's our turn. We can't let Patrick's death be for nothing."

"You don't have to convince me," she said. "I'm all for fighting back. I just don't think we should go in blindly. We need a plan."

"It's impossible to plan for something like this," Vince said. "We have no idea what we're dealing with. The City could be a town of ten or an army of thousands. There are too many variables. For all we know, the City doesn't even exist."

"Let's hope that's not the case," Rupert said, "otherwise we're stranded out here in the middle of nowhere."

"Stranded?" Ella asked. "This boat will get us back to shore in no time."

As these words left her mouth, the low hum of whatever propelled the boat went silent. The vessel slowed until only the gentle waves pushed it forward. She covered her mouth, as if her words had caused the malfunction.

Alan entered the room. "What happened? Why did we stop?"

Vince shrugged. "I don't know. There must be something wrong."

Alan threw his arms up in the air. "Well, that's just perfect. Now we're stranded in the middle of the ocean."

"We're not stranded," Ella said. "We just have to figure out what's wrong, and fix it."

"How in the world are we going to do that? This technology is way beyond our understanding. It took us long enough just to get the boat started, and that's when it was working properly."

"We still have to try." She turned to Vince. "Right?"

"We should try. Saul is in critical condition. If we stay out here too long, he'll die."

They could hear Saul coughing from the other room. Alan looked back. "Damn it. Okay. I'll keep an eye on him. You guys get out there and figure out what's going on." He trotted out to tend to Saul.

Ella grabbed Vince and pulled him out the door. "Let's get to it."

"I'll stay up here," Rupert said, "in case Alan needs help."

Ella and Vince went back through the lounge, down the spiral stairs, and past the pantry. There was a hatch in the floor near the very back of the boat. Ella crouched down and pulled. It did not budge. "It's locked."

Vince stood beside her as she struggled with the hatch, but he was too distracted to help. He stared off to the left, out to the water. "Woah…" he muttered.

Ella looked up. "What's wrong?"

"There's something over there."

She looked. "I don't see anything."

"It's there. I feel the energy."

"Energy? You mean someone else is out there? Another boat?"

"It's a strong energy. Maybe more than one person. But it feels different."

"Different how?"

"It doesn't feel like multiple people. It feels like one source."

"How is that possible?"

"Whatever it is, it lives for a long time. Barnabus lived for as long as I did. Longer even. When we were in that cave, I could feel his strong energy. This feels similar. It may be someone from the City. It may even be the City itself." He looked back down to the hatch, pulled out his knife, and spun the handle to face her. "Here, use this."

She took the knife and dug it into the thin cracks along the edge of the hatch. Vince knelt down and grabbed the door handle. He looked to her to see if she was ready. She nodded. He pulled up as she pried open. The door cracked and then popped free. Inside was a mess of metal and wires, twisting in every direction. They stood over the hole, staring down at the machinery.

"No wonder this thing goes so fast," Ella said. "They've got some serious stuff going on here. There's no way we can figure this out. The camera took all night. This will take days."

Vince looked over his shoulder, out at the water again. "There's definitely something out there."

"Don't worry about that now. We have to find a way to get this boat moving. Suggestions?"

"I think we should leave the boat behind."

"You want to ditch the boat?"

He pointed to the deck. "We have all of these wooden planks, and we brought plenty of rope. We can build a raft and paddle the rest of the way."

Ella's face was cynical.

"We have to get there somehow, and we don't have time to fix whatever this is," he said, pointing to the hatch.

"If that energy *is* the City, we'll have no problem paddling over there."

"But if it isn't, we're stuck in the water with nothing left. We can't fit our equipment on a raft. We'll run out of food."

Saul screamed from the second floor. "Vince!"

He popped up and dashed towards the stairs. "There's no time to argue about this, Ella. Saul is going to die. Whatever is out there, it could help him. I know there's a risk, but we have to try."

Ella ran along his side, climbing up the stairs. "Whatever you decide, I'm with you."

They ran through the lounge back to the bedroom. Saul was hysterical, screaming and twisting about. Alan and Rupert were trying to restrain him. Vince rushed in to help. "We have to calm him down."

"How?" Alan asked.

"I don't know, but he's going to hurt himself." Without warning, he passed out again. His body went limp, and he flopped back down onto the bed. Vince hovered his hand over Saul's chest. "He's weak. I can just barely feel his energy."

Ella placed her hand on his shoulder. "It's your call. Stay here or build the raft?"

He looked at Saul's unconscious face. "Let's build the raft."

Alan looked up. "Raft?"

Ella nodded. "There is something or someone out there on the water. Vince can feel its energy. It might be the City. Right now this boat is useless. But there are wooden boards down there on the deck, and we have plenty of rope. We can build a raft and paddle the rest of the way."

Alan clapped his hands together. "Sounds like a plan. Let's get moving."

They went out on the deck and started prying up the floorboards, building a pile in the middle. When they had enough, they unpacked the rope and started tying them together. Vince showed them, and they followed his technique. Within an hour, they had a functional raft, big enough to fit all of them.

Vince and Ella went back upstairs for Saul. They moved him back onto the stretcher and carefully carried him down. They tied off the raft and threw it overboard. It began to float away, but the rope yanked it back towards them. Rupert climbed down first to help with Saul. He took the stretcher from Vince, and he gently laid it down near the back. Once Saul was safely on the raft, Ella and Vince climbed down, each holding extra boards for paddling.

Alan looked down to them. "Hold on one second. I'll be right back." He left, and when he came back, his arms were filled with food from the pantry. He passed them down one by one. "Might as well take some food, right?"

Rupert grabbed the boxes and placed them in the middle. "Good thinking."

Alan climbed down and squeezed on with the rest of them. Vince drew his knife. "Ready? Do we have everything?" They all nodded. He swung his arm and chopped the rope. They floated away from the boat, into open waters. Vince pointed ahead. "It's over there. The energy. We need to go that way." They each took a board and started paddling.

The sun beat down through the clear sky. They shed their coats as sweat began to drip from their faces. They panted in unison with each stroke of the paddles. Ocean salt splashed up and stained their skin. The cool breeze had stopped, leaving them with stale air. They all struggled. All except Vince.

Alan stopped to rest for a moment. "How do you keep up that pace, Vince? It's way too hot out here for this."

"You're not used to the heat yet. The transition from Snow Peak must be jarring. I've seen much worse than this."

Ella pointed up ahead. "Look." Emerging in the distance was a small mass of land. "It looks like an island."

Rupert shaded his eyes. "That's one small island."

Vince nodded. "Yes, very small, but the energy I feel is incredibly intense."

Saul lifted his weak hand and reached towards the island.

"You feel it too, don't you Saul?"

Saul nodded and tried to speak, but his words came out soft and slurred. "I feel it, Vince. It's a beautiful feeling, to know that an energy that strong can exist." He lowered his arm to his side. "The pain is gone, and that terrifies me. I'm not ready to die."

Vince's eyes began to water. "We'll get you help. We'll save you."

"It's okay, Vince. I know you tried, but there's no one on that island that can help me."

"Don't say that. There is someone on that island. They'll help you. They have to help you. If they don't, I'll make them!"

Saul laughed. "You were never the aggressive type, Vince. I know I didn't show it when we were kids, but that's something I've always admired about you. You care for others. You stand up for the weak. You stick to your principles." He coughed. Blood dripped from his lips and down his cheek. Vince leaned forward to hear his next words. "You always find hope where there's none to be found, but I'm afraid for me there is no more hope." His eyes rolled back, and his breath stopped. Vince still felt a glimmer of life, but it was fading fast.

Ella pointed to the island again. "Vince, look."

Vince glanced over and saw a giant tortoise crawling onto the shore. Without a thought, he picked up Saul's body and dove into the water.

He wrapped Saul's arms over his shoulders he swam towards land, leaving the raft behind. He kicked his legs and paddled his arms, exerting all of his energy. His chest pumped with adrenaline as he raced through the water. There was no time to rest. No time to think. This was his last chance to save Saul.

He reached the shore and collapsed in the sand, Saul falling beside him. The waves crashed over them as they lay on the ground. He glanced at Saul's almost dead eyes and forced himself to get up, dragging Saul along the sand. The giant tortoise had walked up the beach and was heading towards a patch of grass. The hot grains shifted beneath Vince's wet feet. His toe caught a rock, and he stumbled over face first. When he got back up his face was covered with sand. He grabbed Saul and kept on marching.

When they reached the tortoise, he collapsed beside it. The creature ignored him. Vince hovered his hand over the rough shell and felt the pulsing energy. He grabbed Saul's hand and pressed it again the surface. "Come on Saul!

Drain!" A tear ran down his face. "I know you're still there. I know you can feel it." Saul didn't move. "Don't give up on me, damn it. Drain!" He shook Saul's shoulders until his eyes peeked open. A confused, delirious daze washed over his face. Vince pointed to the tortoise. "Saul! Drain! Now!"

Saul looked over, reached his hand out, and leaned against the shell. The tortoise let out a loud moan, reacting to the touch of Saul's skin. It pulled away, but Saul leaned in with it. Its legs gave out, and it fell to its stomach, squirming around in pain. It retracted its head into the large shell. Sounds of death chimed from within until finally all noise and movement stopped.

Saul's hand dropped to the ground as he fought off a coughing fit. Vince patted his back. "There you go. Just breathe." He looked into his eyes again and saw life. "Are you okay?"

Saul grabbed his stomach. "I think so." He lifted his shirt to see the healed wound. In its place was a deep red scar. "It still hurts, but it's better."

The raft reached the shore, and the others ran up the beach. Alan reached them first. When he saw that Saul was okay, he ran up and squeezed him in his arms. Confused, Saul tilted his head at Vince. Alan let go and stepped back. His cheeks turned a rosy red. "Sorry," he said. "You don't know me." He stuck out his hand. "My name is Alan."

Saul grabbed his hand and firmly shook. "Nice to meet you, Alan."

"You saved my life. I couldn't be more grateful."

Ella and Rupert came up behind him. Rupert stepped up and shook his hand next. "I'm Rupert. This is Fred. It's a pleasure to meet you. Vince has told us much about you."

"Not too much, I hope."

"We know your past. We know what you went through in Rodin. But you seem to have turned around. It's good to see you're on our side."

Lastly, Ella shook his hand. "Ella. Glad you're doing better. You were getting pretty bad, but it looks like that drain did the trick. You're all healed up."

Saul scanned across all the new faces. "You know about draining?"

Rupert nodded. "Vince told us."

Vince looked at the giant tortoise shell. "Ella, the giant tortoise can live for over two hundred years."

They all laughed.

Alan looked past Vince and pointed. "Guys, look." They turned their heads, and in the distance, at the very edge of the horizon, there was a wall. It was a great distance away, stretching far off in both directions. "Do you think that's the City?"

Saul squinted. "Looks like an outer border. A wall to keep outsiders like us out."

"That's the border?" Ella said in disbelief. "The City must be huge."

Vince nodded. "Bigger than I anticipated." He looked to the setting sun. "Come on, let's get moving. The day's almost gone. If we leave now, we can get there by morning."

They walked to the raft and pushed out into open waters. Vince and Saul paddled while the others slept. They did not know what dangers awaited them, but they knew they would face them together. They drifted towards the unknown. Towards the City. Towards Victor Greene.

AGE OF END:
KINGS AND CROWNS
PREVIEW CHAPTER

ONE

THERE WAS A room, walls lined with monitors. Screens on top of screens, side by side, emitting an aura of video footage. In the center of the room, sitting on a rolling chair, was Charlotte.

Her eyes were glued to the wall of monitors. She watched in amazement as Vince and the others sailed across the ocean. She was fascinated by the events in the cave. She knew Barnabus was a loose cannon, but slaughtering everyone in the cage? Greene would not be pleased. And now Vince and Saul were on their way. She scribbled notes into her journal, keeping track of everything.

A man popped his head in the room. "It's happening again. More bombings."

"More?" she said. "Christ, Trevor. Sometimes I just don't know about this world. Do you think we're safe?"

"Oh yeah. There's no way they're getting through the walls. Anything interesting happen in here?"

Charlotte leaned back in her chair. "You have no idea. Barnabus is dead. Vince shot him with his own gun."

"I can't say I'm surprised. It was bound to happen at some point. The man got stabbed in the eye on his first assignment. He was careless. Always has been."

"He had it coming, too. That crazy son of a bitch slaughtered all of Greene's subjects. Dismembered them in the cage."

"Holy crap! I've talked to him a few times. He did seem a little off his rocker."

"I know, right? He gave me the creeps."

"But your name sounds so similar to his."

"Ugh, don't remind me. Marble was such a pleasant last name until I met Barnabus Carbul, weirdo of the century. I don't know why Greene likes him so much."

"They go way back. They've been working together for a long time. He's about as loyal as they get."

"Until he snaps and goes on a murdering spree."

Trevor chuckled. "Yeah, well, not everyone's perfect."

Charlotte glanced back at the wall of screens. "Anyway, now Vince, Saul, and the others are headed this way. They took his boat and their sailing across the ocean right now. They say they're going to stop Greene. Saul's pretty injured, too. Barnabus shot him. I think he's going to die."

"Wow. You've seen some exciting stuff these last few days."

"Jealous?"

He smiled. "Cosmetic test subjects aren't nearly as exciting. You really lucked out getting assigned to the vitality sector."

"Luck had nothing to do with it. I worked hard to get where I am."

"I know. I'm just teasing you."

A rumble came from outside. Charlotte turned. "Are you sure we're safe? Those bombs sound close."

"There are three walls around the Spire, all armed with cannons. We'll be fine. That's probably just our guys firing back."

The lights in the room turned red, and the alarm blared over the speakers. A loud automated voice called out. "Potential spire breach. Secure all data and proceed to your designated safe room."

Charlotte took one last look at the screens against the wall, hit the record button, and grabbed her journal. "So much for safe. Think we'll finally get to use the evacuation pods?" She walked through the door.

Trevor followed as they walked down the hall. "The alarm sounds if they breach the first wall. They've still got two more to go. There's no way that will happen. It never has before."

"You never know. Simon is resourceful."

"Simon is a crazy terrorist with a messed up sense of justice. He plays dirty."

"Even more reason to take this seriously."

Trevor shrugged. "I am taking it seriously. I'm just confident in Greene's security."

"You shouldn't be overconfident. It leads to embarrassment."

"There's nothing wrong with being confident."

"There is if it gets you killed. That's how Saul got shot. He didn't think Barnabus would do it. But when it comes to people like Barnabus, or Simon, you always proceed with caution. There's no telling what they'll do. The crazy are unpredictable."

"Where does Greene fall on your crazy-scale?"

She looked around to see if anyone was listening, and then lowered her voice. "I don't believe in everything Greene stands for, but the man has principles, and he sticks to them. I respect that. Simon is just a savage."

They turned the corner and headed towards the safe room at the other end of the hallway. "You don't believe in what he stands for, huh? This is the first time I'm hearing this."

"Keep your voice down. It's not really something I want to advertise. I probably shouldn't have even mentioned it."

"You're right, you shouldn't have. That kind of talk will get you fired. Or thrown in prison."

"I wouldn't get thrown in prison."

"You would. Have you seen the cell room? Do you have any idea how many of those people committed treason?"

"But those are terrorists. Members of the Crowns. He wouldn't lock one of his workers up with them."

"Are you sure about that? I've never met the man, but I hear he can hold a grudge."

"Just don't mention this to anyone else and I won't have to worry."

"My lips are sealed."

They reached the end of the hall and entered the safe room. Everyone else was already there. "Took you long enough," said the man in front. "We've been waiting. You know there are terrorists out there, right? You could have picked it up a little."

Charlotte sighed. "Calm down. They won't even make it past the second wall." She pressed the red button and the door locked behind her.

To Be Continued in...

Pick up *Kings and Crowns* today to find out what happens to our heroes in the City. For more information, visit:

www.tothemoonpublish.com/kings-and-crowns

Or pick up *Age of End: The Complete Set* to get all three books:

www.tothemoonpublish.com/age-of-end-complete-set

Want More?

For news on upcoming books, sign up for Moon Mail at:

www.tothemoonpublish.com/moon-mail

Did you leave a review?

Written reviews greatly help a book get noticed. If you enjoyed this book and would like to help me out, please leave a review and let others know about the series. Thank you for supporting me!

About The Author:

Chris Yee grew up in Needham, Massachusetts. As a young child, he had a wild imagination, thinking up stories of mystery and wonder. People would ask what he wanted to be when he grew up, and the answer was always the same. He wanted to be an author. As he grew older, educational interests pulled him away from the world of writing and into math and science. He attended Northeastern University and received a Bachelor's Degree in civil engineering. He now works in Boston, full-time as an engineer. Despite his technical background, he never lost an interest in writing. He writes every day, to fulfill a passion that has never faded.

www.ingramcontent.com/pod-product-compliance
Lightning Source LLC
Chambersburg PA
CBHW021008120726
47905CB00009B/2907